W9-BFB-893

SPEED
of LIGHT

HIGH SCHOOL

LIBRARY

SPEED of LIGHT

BUSSELTON SENIOR HIGH SCHOOL
X 423151
F
COW
LIBRARY

JOY COWLEY

GECKO PRESS

This edition first published in 2014 by Gecko Press
PO Box 9335, Marion Square, Wellington 6141, New Zealand
info@geckopress.com

Distributed in New Zealand by Random House NZ
Distributed in Australia by Scholastic Australia
Distributed in the United Kingdom by Bounce Sales & Marketing

© Joy Cowley 2014
© Gecko Press Ltd 2014

All rights reserved. No part of this publication may be reproduced
or transmitted or utilized in any form, or by any means, electronic,
mechanical, photocopying or otherwise without the prior written
permission of the publisher.

A catalogue record for this book is available from the
National Library of New Zealand.

Gecko Press acknowledges the generous support of
Creative New Zealand

Cover by Keely O'Shanessey, New Zealand
Typesetting by Luke & Vida Kelly, New Zealand
Edited by Patricia Lee Gauch
Printed in China by Everbest Printing Co Ltd,
an accredited ISO 14001 & FSC certified printer
ISBN paperback: 978-1-877579-93-6
ISBN e-book: 978-1-927271-23-0 (epub);
978-1-927271-24-7 (mobi)

For more curiously good books, visit www.geckopress.com

To Patti Gauch who is a fine author,
good friend and superb editor:
thank you for this trinity of gift.

– Joy

CONTENTS

1

WIND VELOCITY: *Wind speed is accurately measured by an anemometer; but there is an older way of estimating wind force by observing its effect on the environment. The 13-grade Beaufort Scale measures wind from 0 ("Calm", at 2 km/h) to 12 ("Hurricane", at over 119 km/h). Number 10 on the Beaufort Scale is "Storm", with 100 km/h winds and 9-metre waves. In a storm, trees can be uprooted and damage to buildings is likely.*

The house had been built on the highest point, its snout over the sea, sniffing every change in the weather. If you stood against the low front wall, you had no awareness of the earth beneath, only sky and, far below, a blue bathtub of harbour floating toy boats. Like a space station, Jeff thought, like a glass and concrete laboratory, not a house, no, nothing house-like except the furniture that came from their old place. They had moved nine plus four months ago but he still felt he needed permission to open the smooth black cupboards in the kitchen. No catches. A magic touch with a finger and they sprang open, surprising you with ordinary things like orange juice and cans of tomato soup.

At this height, he could see weather from any direction long before it arrived, high clouds shredded by wind, or fat cumulus rolling in from the Hutt Valley, pencil lines of rain scribbling their way over the eastern hills. Today, though, brought something new. Jeff had never seen anything like it, this army of cloud, as dark as an oil slick, coming up from the South Island, blackening land and sea. The harbour was still calm, sunlit water offering no kind of warning, but out in the strait the shadow was dense and picking up water in white patches.

Eddie the new gardener was preparing for the change in the weather, putting the barbecue table and chairs in the shed. Jeff liked the way Eddie walked, rolling from side to side without a sound. Elephants walked like that because they had soft pads on their feet. Eddie had red canvas shoes without ties.

"Will it be a bad storm?" Jeff asked.

"Little beauty," said Eddie, folding a wooden chair. "Sea will be across the road high tide tonight. You going anywhere?"

"No."

"Just as well. Road might be closed. If you like you can tie that cover down over the barbecue. Good and tight, mind you."

"Sure." Jeff tugged at the padded canvas cover. "Hey, I want to ask you something: is your real name Eddie?"

"About as real as it gets. Why?"

He laughed. "Our names are the same! We're both nines!"

"What?"

"Jeff and Eddie add up to nine and nine is the perfect number!"

Eddie stood still, hugging the chair, his mouth open under a thin moustache. "Huh?"

"Nine is my number," Jeff explained. "It's yours, too. Look, E is the fifth letter in the alphabet, D is four, I is nine. Add those up. Eddie. Five, four, four, nine and five make twenty-seven. Then you add the two and the seven together. What have you got? Nine."

"If you say so."

"Eddie, it's about numerology. My brother told me. Numbers tell us who we are. Seven is the spiritual number. I forget what eight is, but nine, powerful nine means perfection."

"You got me there, kid." Eddie shifted the chair to scratch behind his ear. "I'm not what you'd call a number nerd."

"It's really very simple. The letters for Jeff are ten and five and six and six. Twenty-seven for Jeff. Two and seven make —"

"Isn't your name Jeffrey?"

He shook his head. "I prefer Jeff because Jeff is nine and nine is my number." But he knew from the blank stare that Eddie was not taking it in. There was a stirring in the air, like the movement of a propeller.

The big gardener shifted sideways to look at the sky. "Gotta get these chairs in the shed. Reckon your old man'll be back any time soon. Don't forget the barbecue cover."

Jeff watched him lumber around the side of the house, pants hanging low, a map of sweat stains on the back of his T-shirt. Another air movement rustled some dry leaves near the swimming pool. The gum tree beside the bronze gates shivered and a blob of wetness burst into a star shape on the concrete. Another. Then another. Rain was arriving ahead of the cloud, water drops from a blue sky, and with it came the sound of the Lexus, the hush of tyre tread in the gravel and a groan as the electronic gate released itself, swinging inwards.

His father Winston was home. Winston was a six.

As Jeff ran through the southern wing of the house, he realised how dark the sky had become, a summer afternoon suddenly evening. He felt the wind;

saw Eddie outside, struggling with the shed door; heard the rattle of large raindrops; then he was skidding the hall mat along the marble floor and tumbling, arms outspread, into his bedroom. He wrenched open his backpack.

His father didn't like him talking to the gardener.

"Jeffrey?" The front door opened. "You there, Jeffrey?"

"Doing homework, Dad," he called.

Winston Lorimer stepped into the room. "Good lad. Where's your mother?"

"I don't know."

"And your sister? Andrea?"

Jeff shrugged. "Eddie said Mum went to pick up Andrea from college. That was ages ago." He glanced at his father.

"Shopping, no doubt," said Winston. "Women, huh? They know every shoe shop in the city. She's not answering her phone." His smile disappeared. "I said she's not answering her phone!"

"Andrea can't take her phone to school. There's a rule about −"

"Your mother! I'm talking about your mother's phone! There's a helluva storm coming up, eighty knot wind gusts, they reckon. It's going to be dangerous out there and −" He stopped and wiped the back of his hand across his forehead. He'd had a haircut. It was grey stubble, close to his scalp.

"Mum phoned Eddie and asked him to put away the garden furniture." Jeff put down his pen. "Do you think it'll be that bad?"

"So she talked to the blimp, did she? What else did she say?"

"His name is Eddie," Jeff murmured.

Winston gave a short laugh. "Eddie, blimp, tinkerbell – take your pick." Then he shook his head. "There was a warning on the car radio. Stay away from coastal roads at full tide! Don't go over the Rimutaka hill. Make sure boats are securely moored. God help us! Women can be so impractical! I'm worried about her! You know tonight's ferry sailings are cancelled."

"Dad, they'll be okay. They'll be home before dark." But it was already dark, not night dark but an angry day dark that threw rain like handfuls of nails against the window. He switched on the desk lamp. "Mum's a good driver."

His father took another step into the room and looked at his desk. "What's the assignment?"

"Fractions."

"You and your precious numbers." He scrubbed Jeff's hair with his knuckles. "What's it to be? Stephen Hawking the second? Lorimer and Son, Chartered Accountants?"

"I don't know, Dad."

"You must have given the future some thought."

Jeff wished he would go away. "Well, no, I haven't."

"When I was your age, I absolutely knew what I wanted to be. A diver. Did I tell you that?"

Of course he'd told him that. Many times.

"It was those Jacques Cousteau films. Before your time. One minute they were on the sea, plain old waves. The next minute, gliding above another world. I wanted to do that. I wanted to discover underwater volcanoes and new species of fish. I bought a snorkel and mask −" He was interrupted by a gust of wind that slapped the window, rattling it in its frame. After a pause, he gathered words again. "Fortunately, my old man sorted me out."

It seemed odd that his father should think that fortunate. "Mum says Grandpa Lorimer used to beat you with his belt doubled over."

Winston actually laughed. "Kids don't always know what is best for them," he said. His expression changed. "Why doesn't she answer her phone!"

"Honestly, Dad. They'll be all right."

"Yeah, yeah." He turned in the room as though uncertain of direction. "Where's the blimp? Gone home early?"

"He's probably gone by now." Jeff drew a large nine on his paper and filled its loop with dots. "He put all the outdoor furniture in the shed − and the pot plants. He said it's going to last three days." He looked up. "What about the plane tomorrow? Your Mr Jones?"

"Mr Staunton-Jones," his father replied. "No problem. It's an international flight, big aircraft. He'll be here, rain or shine." His smile came back, broad this time. "Good news, Jeffrey, bloody good news, pardon my French, all thanks to our friend Mr Staunton hyphenated Jones. Mark my words! This is the big one! A man can sit counting beans day in, day out, or he can get off his chuff and use a little initiative, do something with his life. How would you like your own island in Fiji?"

"No." Jeff frowned. "I wouldn't."

His father laughed. "Dumbo! It was a rhetorical question about choice. Fiji, a villa in Tuscany, a condominium in Hawaii! This is what Warren Staunton-Jones is offering us. The plain truth, son, is that you can sit here adding up your numbers, or you can make them work for you. Remember that, Jeffrey. The world can be your oyster."

The words formed a hard shell around a memory, and Jeff saw himself aged eight, and his older brother Beckett with a laugh full of sunshine, saying, "The world's my oyster, kid!" The old pain came back, slicing through his stomach so intensely that he thought he might cry.

He missed Beckett. He missed his brother more than anything in the world. He tried to swallow back the tears but they came anyway.

"How do you think I got this house?" his father

said. "Counting beans? One and one make two? How did I —" He stopped. "What's wrong?"

There was another burst of rain against the window. Jeff shook his head.

"What is it, son? Tell me!"

"Nothing, Dad. Nothing. I was — thinking of Beck."

For a moment, rain was the only sound, then his father said those words again. "Beckett is dead."

Jeff thought there might be a replay of the old anger, on and on about the disgrace, the shame, the damage to the Lorimer family's reputation. It didn't happen because at that moment, Winston's cellphone sounded its jazz piano ring, and it was out of his pocket to his face, and he was bellowing with relief, "Where the hell have you been?"

Jeff's mother Helen and his sister Andrea were on their way home.

* * *

Jeff knew he could rely on numbers. They were the only things in the universe that did not change. Multiply any number by an even number and the answer for all eternity was another even number. One million years ago. Two million years in the future. The same. Divide any number by nought and the answer was nothing. Multiply any number by nought and the answer was nothing. But it was in addition and subtraction that a round fat zero showed its muscle. Add a nought to a number and abracadabra, it increased by a factor of ten. Subtract a nought from a number with noughts, and you cut the number down to one-tenth its original size.

He had been six when he'd discovered the power of zero and he still saw it as magic. Not Paul. Paul Fitzgibbon, who sat next to him in school, was a mathematical acrobat who could add up columns of figures upside down on a shop counter and come to a total faster than a machine. Yet Jeff didn't talk to Paul about the magic. Numbers were just numbers, said Paul, who did not see past black marks on paper to the great mystery that kept the universe in order.

Mystery was how Beckett described it that day at the Carter Observatory. It was Jeff's ninth birthday, and he and his brother were lying on their backs in the dark, looking at stars projected on the ceiling, and Beck talked in his laughing voice. Was he laughing? Maybe not. Maybe Jeff just remembered him as always laughing. Beck was telling him how special nine was, how nine was seen as the number of perfection in many religions. Multiply any set of digits by nine, add the numbers in your answer, and they will always come out as nine, he said. They tried it, lying there under the constellation of Orion: two nines are eighteen, one and eight is nine.

Thirty-seven times nine make three hundred and thirty-three. Three and three and three are nine. The excitement of discovery made Jeff's heart beat in his ears, blood tapping like fingers against his mind. This is what he was, nine the perfect number, and then Beckett, already more than two nines older, had whispered, "If you love numbers, they will take you to God."

After the tragedy, Jeff had told his mother about that. She had looked past him into some far-off distance. "He loved drugs, more like it," she said, not allowing her voice to sound sad.

The name Helen was eight, and Andrea was seven, in a family of six, seven, eight and nine.

Beckett was not part of the sequence. As Beck or Beckett he was a three, and three was a prime number that was always a part of nine. Jeff drew a row of nines on his paper and put a three in each of the loops.

* * *

Jeff's side of the house caught the southerly winds. The building was solid, so there was no movement, merely noise and plenty of it, rages of rain hurled at the blackened windows, backed by sounds further out, wind roared in trees, creaks, the crash of someone's dustbin or wheelbarrow. Inside the house, all rooms lit with a peaceful glow. It was like being in a strong lighthouse in a tsunami, quiet walls with chaos outside.

The other wing of the house, facing north, was parent country where Helen and Winston had their bedroom, the gym, their offices set up with swivel chairs and broadband, the TV room they called The Theatre. No exaggeration. It was a theatre, huge screen, surround sound and leather chairs. In a reckless moment, Jeff had told kids at school that their new house had its own movie cinema. Some believed him. The others just laughed. A locked gate meant there weren't any unplanned visits, so his friends had no factual evidence. Winston had promised he could get a couple of DVDs and bring the whole class up for a movie night, but it hadn't happened and now Jeff got tired thinking about it.

Andrea's bedroom was opposite his, but at this moment she was in the kitchen with their mother, their voices coming through with the storm noise so it all sounded like an orchestra tuning up, making no sense at all. Every now and then, Jeff heard his father's belly laugh. Dad would be having his whisky – his family was safe and he was looking forward to tomorrow's visit from his Australian friend, that old Mr Warren Staunton-Jones. They were going to be business partners. Jeff didn't know what the investment was. While Winston said a lot of things like "Pot of gold!" and "Opportunity of a lifetime!" he kept all the details to himself; but he'd flown to Sydney twice, and last month Mr Staunton-Jones had come to Wellington to have dinner at the house, food cooked by a chef from Vérité Restaurant. Jeff remembered two things about that evening: the chef complaining because their knives were blunt, and Mr Staunton-Jones saying he wished Jeff was his grandson, smart nipper like that. Jeff thought the visitor's remark meant he would be included in the after-dinner discussions; but he was wrong. He and Andrea did the dishes.

*　*　*

The wall TV in the dining room brought the storm inside, with images of wet lights and drenched reporters. A road was closed with a van turned over in the wind. Sheets of iron peeled off houses. Jeff couldn't hear what was being said, but the pictures connected with the noise outside, especially the scene at the marina where the masts of yachts waved like conductors' batons.

"Poor devils." Winston raised his glass. "Makes you thankful for a solid haven."

It was pizza again tonight, but Jeff liked pizza and Andrea, who was still in her college uniform, had made a salad for the table. Andrea was seventeen and she looked older, more like Helen's sister than daughter. That's how they acted together, too, sharing thoughts in looks and smiles that sometimes made Jeff feel lonely because he couldn't do that with Winston.

"Hi, Squidgy!" Andrea put a plate on the table. "How was school today?"

"Don't know," Jeff said. "I didn't ask it."

"Why not?" She tapped him on the nose. "It could have been your last opportunity to have a meaningful conversation. Goodbye, school, nice knowing you. Tomorrow, you could be whirled away to the land of Oz."

"Oz?" Winston picked up on the last word.

"Not Oz across the Tasman, Dad. Oz as in wizard, as in Dorothy, as in red shoes."

Winston looked at Helen. "What's she on about?"

But Helen was watching the TV screen, a slice of pizza halfway to her mouth.

A siren cut through the storm noise, only there was no way of knowing if it was from the TV or outside. It was an indecisive sound, frayed by the roar of the rain-soaked wind. Jeff felt Andrea move behind him and lean over, her hair against his neck, her breath warm at his ear. Her voice was so soft that it could not have gone anywhere else in the room. "I've had a letter from Beck," she whispered. "I'll show it to you tomorrow."

2

NUMEROLOGY has a history that goes back 10,000 years. It is part of Greek, Egyptian, Babylonian, Hebrew and Chinese traditions. The Chaldeans, Mayans, Tibetans, Phoenicians and Celts also used systems of numerology to understand nature. The numerology we know today is based on the work of the Greek mathematician Pythagoras, who believed that each number from 1 to 9 represents a universal principle. It is said that these numbers have vibrations that represent all stages of evolution. Significant numbers are birth dates and names.

Jeff knew he had dreamed of his brother, but the moment he opened his eyes, details of the dream were destroyed by two words that came large into his head. Barbecue cover! He sat up in bed and lifted the edge of the curtain. It was morning. The wind and rain were less, but the yard was a mess of drowned leaves, twigs, bits of paper and plastic, a piece of corrugated cardboard stuck in the cactus garden. He deliberately hit his head against the window sill and groaned with another pain. He had forgotten his promise to Eddie to tie the cover down!

He ran out in pyjamas and bare feet, through the dining room dark with curtains and still smelling of Winston's cigar, out the glass doors and into greyness, cold rain and mess. He looked around. Leaves, old shopping bags, the lid of an ice-cream container. Where had all this stuff come from? The sky was dark, weighed down by water, and the harbour, the same colour, was full of rolling waves, not a boat to be seen. He walked carefully through the rubbish, and past the pool solid with flotsam — leaves like dirty brown snow, small sticks, an empty orangeade bottle. It would take ages to clean. And there it was, the barbecue, wet but still standing — without its cover.

Eddie had asked him and he'd said yes, then run into the house when he heard the car, not wanting Winston to see him talking to Eddie, and now it was likely Eddie would get fired anyway, because the barbecue cover was brand new, one of those padded jobs, super waterproof, and it would be Eddie's fault because Jeff had let him down.

For a moment he stood breathless, then he had another thought. The new cover was heavy. The wind had lifted it off the barbecue but it couldn't have gone far, not out of the property, surely. It would be okay. Just lying somewhere. He could put it back.

The rain no longer beat the earth. It was a spray that shifted direction with the wind, but it still soaked him to the skin. He walked faster round the pool, searching the concrete boundary. On each side of the house the wall was high, over three metres with metal spikes on top that were supposed to look ornamental. There was a bit of plastic pinned against two spikes, but no sign of the barbecue cover. He walked on, past the shed, around the corner of his bedroom, and then he stopped.

Near the gate, a eucalyptus branch had broken. It hadn't come off the tree but was hanging down, a fan of small branches pinning some dark cloth to the concrete. His mind said barbecue cover. He wanted it to be that, but he knew the stuff under those gum leaves was the wrong colour.

Closer, it looked like a bag of rubbish that had blown over the wall and landed under the tree, spilling trash.

Rain drifted against his face, and there was a strange feeling in his ears, a swelling, popping sensation as though there had been a sudden change in pressure. He swallowed to clear it, and walked to the tree.

He saw a white foot, shining wet, sticking out from the leaves.

He didn't breathe, didn't think. It seemed the wind and rain stopped — time, too — everything frozen like a painting with him in it. Then his body wanted air. He gulped, stepping backwards.

The thing under the gum tree branch was a dead body.

*   *   *

Only Helen put on her dressing gown. The rain glued Winston's tartan pyjamas to his skin and he was having a problem seeing without his glasses. "Jeffrey! Don't just bloody well stand there!" he yelled as he struggled to pull away the branch. "Give us a hand!"

Jeff could see, but couldn't move. The dead thing was an old woman with a head like a skull, wet grey hair sticking to it. Her mouth was open, a turned-down crescent, showing some black-edged teeth, and her eyes, not quite closed, had a wet shine. She was thin, mostly wet cloth, had some sort of coat with a wet pink scarf and trousers wrapped around skinny legs.

The gum tree branch wanted to swing back. Winston held on, his bare feet skidding in the wet, his toes close to the old head. "Jeffrey?" he bellowed.

It was Andrea who ran and grabbed the woman's feet, dragging her away from the branch. The coat and trousers rolled up the body showing grey-white skin.

The head fell sideways and they heard a small, high-pitched squeak.

"She's alive," said Andrea. She leaned over and put two fingers against the wrinkled neck. "Yes! There's a pulse! Call an ambulance!"

But Winston was already on his phone to the police. "I want to report a break-in. A homeless person. What? How the hell would I know? This is a gated property and the gate's still shut."

Andrea looked at her mother. "Ambulance!" she said.

Knowing that the person was alive made a difference to Jeff. The knots of shock in him unravelled, and strength came back to his arms and legs. He ran into the house to fetch a cushion and a blanket, and he even put the cushion under the head when Andrea lifted it up. The wet hair was thin. He could see the scalp with wrinkles above the ears, and there were hardly any eyebrows and eyelashes. The face had folded in on itself, skin tight against bone, but the neck was loose and saggy. Helen opened an umbrella and had Jeff hold it over the woman's face.

"We should take her inside out of the rain," said Andrea.

"No!" said Winston. "She stays here until the police arrive."

"Your father's right," said Helen. "If we move her we might make her injuries worse."

Winston leaned over, until his head was under the umbrella. He shouted, "How! Did! You! Get! In!"

"Sweetie, she can't hear you," said Helen.

"I need to know." Winston's look was urgent. "Are you telling me she got in here on her own? How! Tell me how! It's gang related, I'll bet my life on it. There's a mob of them and she's the decoy."

"Dad, there's no one else here," said Andrea. "Why don't you go and get changed?"

"We're waiting for the police." Winston clenched and unclenched his fists, then he spun around to face Helen. "What's the bet it was that fag gardener! He let her in!"

Helen and Andrea exchanged glances, a shuttered look that Jeff could not interpret, and Helen said to Winston, "Go inside! You have to be at the airport at eleven."

Winston's eyes were wide. "Don't bloody patronise me! My instinct about this is right!" He pointed at the figure on the ground. "She is not some pathetic old homeless lady who got lost. There's a whole lot more to this!"

Helen folded her arms and walked away. Winston also marched off, but not into the house. He was going to search every part of the property, including the basement and the sheds, to see what had been stolen.

The woman on the ground did not seem to be

breathing but Andrea assured Jeff she was still alive. "Actually, her pulse is stronger," she said.

Jeff shifted the umbrella. The air smelled of wet gum leaves. The rain was not heavy now but it was persistent, and drops plopped off the umbrella spokes in a circle around the woman's head. Andrea was kneeling by the woman, but looking up at Jeff. He wanted to talk to her about Beck. He looked over his shoulder to see where his mother was, then he said in an urgent whisper, "Where did you put the letter?"

"Sorry. I left it at school. I'll bring it home tonight, but don't let them see it. It's good news."

"Yeah?"

She smiled. "They're extraditing him. He's coming back to New Zealand."

The umbrella flipped and water poured over his bare feet. "For real?"

"He thinks so. Probably be the new prison near Auckland."

He wanted to run, shout, jump up and down. This was more than good news. It was a miracle. Beck was coming home! He waved the umbrella. "Yay! We'll be able to see him!"

Andrea's head turned, her eyes flickered, her smile disappeared. "No, Squidge! We have to go to school this morning. Dad will be going to the airport to meet Mr Staunton-Jones – won't you, Dad?"

Jeff gulped back his excitement. Winston was immediately behind them, still in his wet pyjamas. Their father's eyes were wide with triumph. He had discovered the barbecue without its cover, evidence that they'd been robbed!

★ ★ ★

When the ambulance and the police car arrived, Winston was the only one still in his pyjamas. He looked like a wet dog, the grey hairs on his chest plastered between the buttons, and when Jeff offered him the umbrella, he pushed it away, as though it would somehow impede the investigation. The police officers, a man and a woman, had their own umbrella, the man holding it and asking questions while the woman made notes on a pad.

Winston was losing patience with the questions, which seemed to Jeff to be a bit pointless. Are you sure none of you have seen this lady before? Did one of you open the electronic gate unintentionally? Could she have been a passenger in your car? Is it possible that the storm caused the gate to default and it opened by itself?

The paramedics took off the wet blanket and put a yellow waterproof sheet over the old woman's body and an oxygen mask over her nose. Kneeling on either side, they peeled away the pink scarf and examined her carefully before putting her on a stretcher. One of the paramedics said to the police officers, "My guess is somewhere between eighty and eighty-eight. No obvious fractures. Hypothermia and maybe concussion. She could have dementia."

The other paramedic said, "Sometimes they wander off and get lost."

"She couldn't get in here without help!" Winston pointed a finger like a gun. "There'll be more of them. Thieving louts! They come from the outer suburbs. That's how they work – in packs."

The male officer looked at his notes. "You said you searched the property and saw no one else."

"They would have got away," Winston argued. "The able-bodied went back over the wall and she was left behind."

"Is there anything missing?"

"No, Officer, there isn't," said Helen.

"Yes, there is, the new cover for the barbecue," Winston said, but he didn't convince anyone, not even himself, and when the officer suggested that it could have blown away in the storm, he didn't reply. Instead he pointed again to the woman who was now on the stretcher and being wheeled towards the ambulance. "Have you searched her pockets?"

"Yes." One of the paramedics opened a wet plastic bag and showed a plastic comb, a lace-edged handkerchief and a sodden pack of indigestion tablets. "No identification," he said.

"She'll be missing somewhere," said the woman officer. "We'll phone around the rest homes."

"All night pinned under that branch!" Andrea said. "How did she survive the storm?"

The paramedic smiled. "Not all night. A few hours, perhaps. We'll get her to the hospital for assessment."

Jeff asked, "Will she get better?"

"Probably. It's hard to tell. It wouldn't be the first time a patient with dementia has wandered off in a storm and got lost. They can get unsettled."

"A storm like this unsettles everyone." The male police officer extended a hand to Winston. "It was a chaotic night. I suggest, sir, that you go inside and get warm, and if you have any further concern, you might like to set your mind at rest by having your electronic gates checked."

"Did you hear that?" said Winston, as they walked back to the house. "Did you listen to the way that bloody young pipsqueak talked down to me?"

"Have a shower, sweetie," said Helen. "Andrea? Jeffrey? Grab your books and a bite to eat. You're going to be late for school."

Winston squelched across the white marble floor. "I'll get to the truth of it if it's the last thing I do! Dementia, my foot! What a load of rubbish!"

Helen picked up her car keys. "Darling! Shower! Your Warren Staunton-Whatsit is halfway across the Tasman and you're not even dressed. I'm off to work."

He turned, his mouth open to say a whole lot more, but Helen had her bag and umbrella and was striding towards the garage.

Jeff climbed in the back of his mother's Audi. Andrea got in the front. The garage door opened on the sodden mess left by the storm, and the car backed out and turned. The white-barked branch of the eucalyptus tree was still hanging, branches on the drive like a giant broom, but everything else about the morning had receded into a dream. The rain had even washed away the tracks of the police wagon and the ambulance.

Helen and Andrea were talking about the man who was flying across from Sydney, neither of them able to remember if he preferred tea or coffee, but Jeff, gazing out at the passing of broken trees and wet earth, could not get the old woman out of his mind. Somehow, she was connected with all the old ladies from childhood fairy tales, the one who lived in a shoe, the one who swallowed a fly, the wild witches from Snow White and Hansel and Gretel. That wasn't logical, of course, but then neither was an elderly woman inside a gate that could not be opened from the outside. He looked at his watch, counting the seconds down the hill to the main street: forty-one, six seconds longer than usual due to debris on the road.

His father could be right. There was more to this than anyone knew, only Jeff was sure it wasn't about vandalism or theft.

★　★　★

Jeff wasn't the only student who was late. Nearly everyone had been affected by the storm and some didn't get in because roads were blocked or trains delayed. There was no damage to the school, but a drain outside the staffroom had blocked, causing a flood that went halfway across the tennis courts, water deep enough for what Mrs Wilson called high jinks. Until she came out and stopped it, some kids were ankle deep, kicking water at those who tried to get by, scoring points when they gave someone a face wash. Jeff got a face wash but he barely noticed it. Too many other things were jostling for attention in his mind.

Paul Fitzgibbon said his uncle's neighbour had a yacht blown off its mooring and onto the rocks at Evans Bay. "Did your place get any damage?"

"Yes." Then he corrected himself. "No. Not really."

Paul looked a question at him.

"There was this weird thing." Jeff stopped, because

now it was so weird, he knew it couldn't have happened – at least, not in the way he had witnessed it.

"Like what?" said Paul.

"We discovered an old lady lying under our gum tree."

"A what?"

"One of the branches fell on her and she was soaking wet. Unconscious. The ambulance came. The paramedics thought she might have dementia, you know, forgotten where she was." Jeff decided not to mention Winston and the police. "They took her to hospital."

"Is she all right?"

"We don't know. It was only this morning I found her. I thought she was dead." A wave of coldness went up his back and shuddered in his shoulders. "We don't know how she got in. The gate was locked and the walls are way too high for climbing. She was really little and thin."

"The storm!" said Paul. "A tornado picked her up and dumped her in your place."

For a second, Jeff thought that possible, then he saw Paul's smile.

"You're kidding," he said.

"Sure I'm kidding." Paul put on his goofy smile, the one where he crossed his eyes, then he asked, "Did you do your patterns of equivalent fractions?"

"What?"

"Homework!"

"Oh, yes." He was glad that the subject had been changed. "Dead easy, wasn't it?"

"Kids' stuff," said Paul.

*   *   *

Jeff liked Mrs Wilson. As teachers went, she was near the top of the okay list, meaning she was interesting and she didn't talk to them as though they were all wearing diapers. True, she tended to get off the subject and ramble a bit, but she had a wacky sense of humour. She laughed at them, and when she got too serious they laughed at her and she was cool with that. Jeff thought they were lucky to have her.

"Right, boys, enough storm talk. Let's pick up on yesterday. What is the world's biggest ocean?"

They all knew, so no one replied.

She smiled. "And how big is the Pacific Ocean?"

"One hundred and sixty million square kilometres," said Jake Kohitolu.

"Thank you, Jake. Actually it's one hundred and sixty-nine point two million square kilometres, but maybe you measured it when the tide was out." She gave him an extra smile. "And the deepest point in the Pacific Ocean?"

"The Mariana Trench near the Mariana Islands," he said.

"Correct. The Mariana Trench north of Australia and south of the Philippines. The deepest ravine in the world! It's two thousand, five hundred and fifty kilometres long, sixty-nine kilometres wide, and its depth – can anyone tell me its maximum depth?"

No one replied. Jeff looked around the room, determined to keep his mouth closed. They were all supposed to know this.

"Would someone like to guess?"

Tawhiri Smallwood put up his hand. "As deep as the Grand Canyon?"

Jeff exploded. "No! The Grand Canyon is eighteen hundred metres deep. The Mariana Trench is ten thousand, nine hundred and eleven metres at its deepest point."

Mrs Wilson beamed with pleasure. "Jeffrey Lorimer, you continue to astound me! How do you remember these figures?"

He shrugged, unable to tell her. It wasn't difficult. The deepest part of the trench came down to Beck's number three. The Grand Canyon was his own number nine.

She opened her computer and put diagrams on the board, comparing the great world rifts. "The Mariana Trench is six times the depth of the Grand Canyon. Imagine the challenge to explorers! Everest had been climbed many times! Men had walked on the moon! But no one got to the bottom of the

Mariana Trench until March 2012. Can you tell me why?"

"Pressure," Paul murmured.

"Exactly," said Mrs Wilson. "Seven hundred and three kilograms per square metre. Imagine what that would do to your ears!"

Jeff stared at the diagrams. Pressure. Ears. That morning, when he'd seen the body under the branch, something had happened to him. It was as though every function in his body had closed down and then, in his ears, had come a swelling sensation, a popping as though he were in a plane coming in to land. He clasped his hands under the desk, tight, to squeeze out the memory. No, it hadn't happened. It couldn't have happened. There was no reason for it.

★ ★ ★

Andrea brought the letter home from school, and he was able read it on the dining room table because both their parents were at the hotel with Mr Staunton-Jones. It was another one-page letter, pencil on thin brown lined paper, faint and not easy to read. Andrea had explained that they weren't allowed to have ball-point pens in prison because those could be used as weapons or to conceal forbidden substances.

"Like drugs?"

"Or needles. Or razor blades."

Beckett's writing had got smaller, which gave Jeff the feeling that his brother was shrinking in that Thai prison, but Andrea said it was probably to get as many words on the page as possible.

They leaned over the paper, picking up each word like some kind of treasure, aware that Beck's hand had shaped them. *Can't tell you how I'm looking forward to coming back. Have the snowmen thawed yet? Or is it still the South Pole? I don't know when it will be but soon, I hope, and I might bring you some souvenirs, cockroaches as big as rats. You'd love that, Andy, and you too, Jeff. But at least we don't need central heating in this place ...*

Jeff looked at his sister. "It's all nonsense. He doesn't say anything real."

"He can't write real things. You have to decode the nonsense, Squidge. He says it's horrible there, hot and vermin infested, and he wants to know if Mum and Dad have changed their attitude or is he still no longer a part of the family. That's what he's saying."

Jeff thought about the weight of his father's statement, *Beckett is dead*. He said it in a heavy way to make sure Jeff and Andrea understood that separation was final.

"They will know, of course," said Andrea. "You can be sure they've been notified that their son is going to serve the rest of his sentence in New Zealand."

"Did they tell you?"

"Of course not. Beck's right. They're made of ice where he's concerned." She folded the page in half and put it back in her media studies book. "You'd never believe he used to be Dad's favourite. Beckett, the golden-haired Adonis! But it's all right, Jeff, they're not going to stop us from seeing him." She said it with such determination that he knew it was going to happen. He wanted to hug her but she was on the other side of the table.

The roar of a chainsaw filled the room, and became high-pitched as the chain bit wood. That was Eddie and François cutting the fallen branch of the gum tree. Eddie had brought in his partner to help with the clean-up and they had found the barbecue cover floating under leaves in the swimming pool. Eddie didn't say anything to Jeff about the cover, just hung it on the deck to dry while he cleaned water out of the barbecue.

Andrea picked up her phone. "You know what? I'm going to phone the hospital again."

"They won't tell you anything."

"So? Let's try something different." She gave him a sly smile as she jabbed in the number. "Hullo? Public hospital? This is Nurse Lorimer speaking. I'm enquiring about an elderly woman admitted by ambulance this morning, suffering hypothermia and amnesia. Thank you. I appreciate that. Is this the intensive care unit? Oh good, I'm Nurse Lorimer enquiring about one of our patients, an elderly woman brought in this morning. Yes, yes. Which ward did you say? Thank you very much." She smiled again at Jeff. "Good afternoon, I'm checking on an elderly woman admitted today. She was found in the storm. Yes. Suffering from hypothermia and – oh. So someone identified her?" Andrea frowned. "She signed herself out? Well, how could that be?" Her voice became less sure. "I'm – I'm a friend, I mean –" She shut down the phone, put her hand on her forehead. "She's gone."

"What?"

"That old woman walked out. She was in a hospital gown, waiting for an x-ray. Then she disappeared. Just vanished. No one knows who she is or where she went."

3

BLACK HOLE: *A black hole is a region of spacetime from which gravity prevents anything, including light, from escaping. Black holes of stellar mass form when stars collapse at the end of their life cycle. After a black hole has formed it can continue to grow by absorbing mass from its surroundings. By absorbing other stars and merging with other black holes, supermassive black holes may form. It is believed that supermassive black holes exist in the centre of most galaxies.*

Saturday morning, the third day of the southerly, wrapped the house in light rain, turning it into a dull cave. Andrea spread the newspaper over the table and read headlines to Jeff – most sporting fixtures cancelled, men out continuing the repair of slips, blocked drains and washouts on the roads, some houses without power, ferry sailings resume, train timetable disrupted for maintenance on rails near Petone. She then passed the newspaper to her brother and took her cereal bowl back to the dishwasher. He watched her shelve the breakfast cereals. Out of school uniform, she looked like one of those chicks from a fashion magazine, skinny white jeans and red boots turned down at the cuffs. Jeff knew she was going out, long before she said it. His sister had two boyfriends, one her parents knew about and one they didn't. Even Jeff had no idea who the other one was, and he was glad he didn't know.

"Any stirrings from the north wing?" she asked.

"I think they're still asleep." He was looking at pictures of storm damage. "They were late. From the noise they made, I guess they had a lot to drink."

Andrea laughed. "Special celebration noise or just normal?"

"Celebration, I think. Dad was singing."

"And I didn't wake up?"

"I did. Mum was trying to shush him but her voice was just as loud. Did that man go back go Sydney?"

"Flew back this morning." She hoisted the strap of her bag over her shoulder. "Will you be all right, Squidgy, if I go to town?"

"Sure. Are you meeting Daniel?"

"We might go to a movie." She smiled. "I'm leaving my phone. It needs recharging."

"Right." He nodded, understanding that it was not Daniel, year twelve at St Pat's, she was seeing. "Have fun."

"I've hidden Beck's letter where they won't find it. I'll take it back to school on Monday."

He nodded again.

She leaned over to hug him and he smelled perfume. "Next Saturday I'll take you to a movie." Then she was gone. He heard her car, the little Toyota Vitz that Winston bought her for her birthday, reverse out of the garage.

He read through the paper to the advertisements. Fifty per cent less fat in a pot of margarine. The statement annoyed him. Fifty per cent less than what? It was frustrating when people deliberately muddied numbers in order to sell something. Clinically proven to be twenty-five per cent more effective. Will make your wash sixty per cent cleaner. You saw it all the time, numbers turned into lies to make money. He turned a page over. Statistics were all right. Graphs were all right. With graphs, numbers worked with change but remained true to themselves. He had invented a name for that. Integer integrity. But still, in his mind, he liked to keep numbers separate from the messiness of life. It meant there was always a place of thinking to go to, an inner room in the mind that was pure and constant.

He folded the paper. It was nearly eleven o'clock.

His parents were still asleep and Saturday cricket had been cancelled. He hated wet weekends. They were so empty. Maybe he would see if Paul was home. The Fitzgibbons had a basement den with a keyboard, a bass, and a Mapex drum kit. Or maybe Paul would want to go down to the indoor skateboard park.

He sat, chin in hands, looking at the glass doors and the cloud that had collapsed around the house as grey mist, so thick he couldn't even see the front wall. Inside, the only sound was the humming of the fridge.

He wasn't as daring as Andrea. If he walked out without telling them, there'd be big trouble. He'd leave a note on the table, and take his phone and the gate opener. He had enough money for a movie if all else failed. Bus or bike?

* * *

He counted the steps down the hill to the bus stop, two hundred and twenty-three to the white house with the friendly German shepherd. He wished he could have a dog like that. Three hundred and ninety-four to the corner of Angus Street where the mist was thin enough to see the harbour, and exactly six hundred and ten to the small glass-sided alcove with wooden seats, bus timetables and about half a dozen people. He took his phone from his jacket pocket and leaned against the glass to text Paul, hoping he hadn't gone to help his father at the timber yard. Could be since the rain was easing. Still a lot of water lying around, and rolling waves in the harbour, but not as wet as yesterday. If not Paul, then who? Maybe Salosa or Ken could be interested in the skateboard park.

Back came a text within a minute. *Yo bro cool see ya P.* Jeff smiled and closed his phone. The Karori bus pulled in and most of the people at the stop got on it. He went inside the shelter and sat on the bench to wait for the bus to the railway station. His mind was full of Paul's new drum kit and an afternoon session in the basement, practising riffs. Right on! Mr and Mrs Fitzgibbon seemed to be deaf to the noise their kids made at the weekend.

Deaf? He touched his ears. That sensation was back, a fullness, not quite pain, behind his ear lobes. He swallowed and there was a popping noise in his head, clearing the hiss of passing traffic. He wondered if he was getting earache again, like when he was a little kid and had to have grommets.

Then someone said, "Hello Jeff."

He turned, realising there was someone at the other end of the seat, saw a woollen hat and pink scarf, dark padded jacket, brown handbag. Between the hat and the scarf were small eyes, dark and shining like chestnuts, and bits of grey hair.

"Hello Jeff, Number Nine."

That was when he saw the mouth, a turned-down crescent, some teeth missing, others blackened at the edges, and he knew, he absolutely knew.

"Thanks for the cushion and the umbrella," she said.

"Are you all right?" It seemed a lame thing to say but it was all he could think of.

"No, I'm not all right." She clutched at her jacket. "I hate this worn-out carcase. You'd think I'd get dumped into something a little more useful, faster maybe. And the timing was atrocious, slap into the worst storm of the year. No, I am definitely not all right but thank you for asking."

Dementia, he thought. She was crazy. Like Mum's Great-aunt Rose who put all the groceries in the washing machine to get rid of germs. He looked directly at the sharp, dark eyes. "How did you get under that tree branch?"

"I don't know. There's always a forgetting. One minute there, next minute here. The reason it was your place was because it's about you."

"About me?"

"Yes, you – and your family. That's why I'm here." She coughed and wiped her mouth on her scarf. "You want me to explain? Some people choose hard paths. Don't get this wrong. Hard paths can be the best teachers, but if you don't pick up on the lessons, you go under. That's when you need help from outside. Or inside, however you see it."

He didn't see it. He didn't see anything. She was a skinny old bird of a woman and he wasn't afraid of her, but her madness had an intensity that made him wish his bus was coming. He looked down the street. "You don't know us," he said.

She laughed like a honking goose. "I know you better than I know this ancient body. Your father's Winston Lorimer, up to his neck in quicksand, mother Helen Lorimer on the edge of a cliff, Beckett in a Thai prison for drug trafficking, Andrea about to leave school, you – do you really want to know about Jeff Lorimer?"

He didn't want to know. "Who are you?" he said.

She opened the clasp on her bag, looked inside. "She was called Maisie, although she was baptised Eleanor May Caldwell, and she lives in a council flat with a yellow budgie. That's as good a name as any." She wiped her nose on her hand. "Who I am doesn't matter. We don't need labels because we have no self. We're the dream-keepers. Isn't this your bus?"

He wanted to ask what a dream-keeper was, but it was his bus, although he was sure she couldn't have seen it from where she was sitting. He stood in front of her for a moment but she had rested her head back and had closed her eyes. Her mouth hung open.

"Goodbye. I'm glad you're not hurt," he said.

She didn't answer.

He climbed on the bus, pressed his pay card against the glass and moved down to the nearest vacant seat. As the bus pulled away from the kerb, he looked back. The bench was empty.

★　★　★

The afternoon was a mess. It wasn't just him and Paul in the basement. One of the younger Fitzgibbons had a birthday and there was a crowd of kids, some belting out old video games on an equally old TV, and the others drumming, arguing and playing table tennis. The parents were all upstairs around the kitchen table, talking and drinking tea, the dog picking up crumbs. It was a nice dog, fat and friendly, and there was a heap of party food. Every now and then the basement door would push open and someone would bring in a plate of cakes or sandwiches. But Jeff's stomach was tight with unease, and even the smell of it turned him off. He sat on a bean cushion in the corner and thumbed through some of Paul's war comics, not really reading them. His mind was like a grasshopper, springing away from the pages and back to the conversation with the woman at the bus stop.

He should have asked her more questions.

He should have remembered everything she said. Now, only two things stuck in his mind, something about his father in quicksand and Andrea leaving school. Well, this was his sister's last year. Of course, she'd be leaving school. How could that be a problem? And quicksand? As far as he knew there was no quicksand in New Zealand. Was that supposed to mean something else? Or was it just gaga talk? If she was crazy, how come she knew their names and that he was Jeff, not Jeffrey, and that he was a number nine?

Paul's cousin Zac had taken over the drums and the noise was out of the tolerance zone. Jeff felt his phone vibrate. It was a text from his mother wanting to know when he would be home. He was going to leave anyway, and Helen's message gave him an excuse to go upstairs and thank Mr and Mrs Fitzgibbon. He said goodbye to Paul and then headed for the station.

On the short train ride, he tuned into quietness, trying to remember more. He came up with very little. He could picture her eyes, like dark beetles, but couldn't recall the words. It had been a short conversation, hadn't it? Was there more to remember? Maisie! She said that! The name was Maisie!

A further thought disturbed him. If he told his parents about the woman at the bus stop, his father would phone the police. They'd have to go through it all over again – and she was just a daffy old woman, not a burglar. Jeff was sure of that.

He would tell his sister. Andrea was safe.

From the railway station, he took a bus that let him off at the bottom of the hill. As he got out, he looked at the bus shelter, wondering if he would see her again. There were only a boy and a girl kissing, and a man talking to a scruffy brown dog. Jeff didn't know if he was disappointed or relieved.

* * *

Winston and Helen had chairs together at the table, and they were leaning together looking at Winston's laptop. She had her hand near his head and was doing that thing with his ear, absent-mindedly stroking it between her thumb and forefinger. When Jeff walked in, they closed the computer and Winston said, "Is Andrea with you?"

"No. I think she went to a movie with Daniel."

"She didn't take her phone," Helen folded her arms.

"It needed recharging." He pointed to the kitchen bench where Andrea's phone was connected with the power point near the toaster. There was something wrong. He was sure they didn't believe him, and he saw that in the look they gave each other. He said in her defence, "She is seventeen. She doesn't need permission to go out with Daniel."

Helen said evenly, "Daniel has phoned several times, trying to contact her."

Winston turned on his fatherly stare. "We are not strict, understand. It is not our intention to turn our children into puppets. But while you live under this roof, you both obey the rules. You say where you are going and what time you will be home."

"I left a note," Jeff said.

"He doesn't mean you," said Helen.

"No, lad. Not you. I'm talking generally. We gave Beckett far too much freedom and look what happened. We won't make that mistake again. There is no doubt in my mind, Mr Staunton-Jones would never have done business with us if he had known I had a drug dealer son languishing in an Asian prison. Never! Warren is an old English gentleman with the highest sense of respectability. He wouldn't allow his property to become tainted by a family with criminal associations." He glanced at Helen.

Jeff was silent. So the old business partner didn't know about Beck.

Helen smiled. "Jeffrey, do you know what he said to your father at the airport? He told us Winston was the son he never had."

"No children of his own, no heirs, poor fellow." Winston spread his hands. "We hit it off from the time we met. I told you, didn't I? When we had the accountants' conference? He was in the Brisbane

Marriott Hotel. He stood out in the crowd, this elderly English gentleman in a grey suit. Distinguished."

Jeff had heard the story many times. "You played golf with him."

"That was in Sydney," said Winston. "The Royal Sydney Golf Club at Rose Bay, would you believe."

Jeff nodded. He was relieved that his father had left off talk about Andrea and Beck, and he leaned forward, trying to show interest. "Will you play golf there again?"

It was Helen who answered, shaking her head. "Mr Staunton-Jones is going back to England. He's got cancer."

"No!" Jeff was sorry. He had liked the man with white eyebrows and wrinkly eyes, who told interesting stories about hunting in Botswana and climbing Mount Kilimanjaro. "We won't see him again?"

"He will certainly live on in our lives," said Winston. He gave Helen a questioning look.

She nodded. "Yes, sweetie. Tell him. We can tell Andrea later."

Winston looked gentle, almost reverent, as he opened the laptop and switched it on. "Jeffrey, you should know this. Our friend has done us a very great favour, one that we will never ever forget."

"We've done him a favour too," Helen put her hand on Winston's arm. "He said that."

Winston picked up his reading glasses. "In 1957 Mr Staunton-Jones bought property at Sydney Harbour for ninety thousand pounds and built a modest house. I have seen it. It's a wide tract of waterfront land, and today it is worth nearly sixty million dollars. It's magnificent!"

Jeff's mouth opened. "He gave it to you?"

"No!" His mother laughed. "We bought it."

Winston leaned forward, "Jeffrey, listen! In Australia they have capital gains tax when you sell assets. It's a big tax, about the same as standard income tax. Now this man was not afraid of hard work. He made a lot of money, paid a lot of taxes. Finally, he said, enough is enough. He refused to sell this land to a property developer. He might have got a big price but a lot would have gone in tax and then what? Someone would build condominiums, ugly high-rise, on the land he loved. So he's allowed us to buy it — wait for it — for one and a half million dollars."

"It has sentimental value," Helen said. "He sees us as his family."

Winston turned the computer around and Jeff saw a plan of some sort, an L-shaped property next to water and something like a tiny postage stamp near a main road. That would be the house. "You've already bought it?"

"It's ours!" His father flung his arms wide. "Signed and sealed!"

"All legal," his mother added. "Nothing dodgy."

Jeff gazed at the plan on the computer. It looked alien and threatening and, for an instant, he imagined it made of quicksand. "We're not going to move to Sydney."

His mother leaned towards him. "No, but we might visit a few times. Wouldn't that be nice?"

"Well, what will you do with it? Rent it?"

"We'll see," she said.

Jeff looked from one to the other. "You're not going to sell it."

"Of course not!" Winston brought his hands together in a clap. "At least, not while our good friend and benefactor is still alive."

So that was it. They were going to sell it to a property developer who would build high-rise, and they'd make heaps and heaps even if they did have to pay capital gains tax. It was what his dad had meant when he said you could count numbers or you could make them work for you.

He knew his parents were disappointed at his lack of enthusiasm but it was difficult to look pleased. He hated change that came without warning, suddenness that unsettled things. It was like living in a horror movie where surprises jumped out at you at every turn and you had to deal with them, somehow making them fit into your life.

He excused himself and went to his room,

opened his maths homework book and flicked through the pages. Prime factorisation. Regular and irregular polygons. Volumes of cubes and prisms. But he couldn't anchor his thoughts. He put his hand over his forehead, wanting to still all the stuff that was going on in there. Too much, far too much! The human brain had about one hundred billion cells. He didn't know who had done the counting but it was impressive. One hundred billion! If every one of those cells was the size of a star, a planet, each human brain would be bigger than an entire galaxy.

At this moment, his head galaxy was totally out of control.

He looked for numbers that he could hold. Three hundred and thirty-three multiplied by three made nine hundred and ninety-nine.

He heard the front door and knew Andrea was home. Poor Andrea. There were voices raised in the kitchen and then Andrea was saying, "Maybe I know more than one Daniel."

He smiled to himself. Good on you, Sis.

A PRIME NUMBER is a natural number greater than 1 that has no positive divisors other than 1 and itself. A natural number greater than 1 that has other divisors is not a prime number but a composite number. The number 5 is prime because only 1 and 5 evenly divide it. The property of being prime is called primality. The smallest prime numbers are 2, 3, 5, 7, 11, 13, 17, 19, 23, 29, 31, 37, 41, 43, 47, 53, 59, 61, 67, 71, 73, 79, 83, 97, 101 ...

Prime numbers have influenced many artists and writers. NASA scientist and author Carl Sagan suggested that prime numbers could be used as a means of communication with aliens.

After the storm came fine autumn days, so clear, so warm, they seemed like compensation for the weather's bad behaviour. Eddie the gardener had cleaned the pool and put out the recliners with cushions, making the yard look like a scene from a travel brochure. One of those Mediterranean places, thought Jeff: swimming pool, tubs of flowers, a little concrete apron out front and, below it, the sea sparkling with light. Even the saw-cut on the eucalyptus tree by the gate had sealed over as though in apology for failure.

Winston had come around to accepting that an elderly dementia patient had wandered in that night, before the gates closed after Helen and Andrea arrived home. There was no other explanation. It was what it had to be. Then the incident was totally eclipsed by the good fortune from across the Tasman. "Water under the bridge," Winston said, patting Helen on the shoulder. "I overreacted about that woman. It was one helluva storm."

Jeff inspected the bus shelter when he biked past, but there had been no sign of the old lady. He told Andrea about Saturday afternoon. She didn't see anything odd in the encounter. "I'm glad she wasn't seriously hurt," she said.

"She knew our names," he insisted.

"Probably. When people are unconscious they hear things. We were standing around her talking to each other – and to the police. Names went back and forth."

He considered that. His sister was so practical that sometimes she could flatten the structures of his thinking with a single sentence. Then he remembered something else. "Beckett! She said his name.

We didn't talk to each other about Beckett."

"Oh yes, we did. I was bending right over her when I told you I'd had a letter from Beck."

She was right. She was always right. He folded his arms and was silent. Then he looked sideways at his sister. "Are you thinking of leaving school before the end of the year?"

"What?"

"I said, are you going to leave school —"

"I heard you! What made you ask such a thing?"

He couldn't say it was the old woman. After all, his ears had felt thick, so he might have misheard her. "I don't know. I just wondered."

"Squidge, you are one strange child! Why on earth would I leave school? It's my scholarship year, right?" She put her hands on his shoulders. "Are you hungry? I am. Get in the car and I'll drive us down for a Chinese meal. It won't take long. We'll be home before the zoo-keepers get back."

He had to laugh. If their parents ever decided they wanted to live in Sydney, then he would stay here with Andrea and life would be good.

* * *

He fished with his chopsticks for the wontons in his bowl of soup, aware of the way some men in the restaurant were staring at his sister. That made him both pleased and uncomfortable. She was eating chicken and cashew nuts, picking the nuts up neatly and popping them in her lipsticked mouth. "Did they tell you about Beck coming back?" she asked.

"No."

"Mum told me. I think she's nervous about him returning to New Zealand."

"Why?"

"Publicity, of course. It'll be in the news, maybe on TV. She and Dad are so phobic." She lifted a piece of chicken and waved it. "They won't stop me from seeing him."

He tried to get the chopsticks around a slippery wonton. "They'll stop me," he murmured.

"We'll work something out. Do you miss him, Squidge?"

He nodded.

"So do I. Remember his jacket pocket? That old khaki jacket and the presents he used to bring home for us? Interesting things like a piece of quartz or obsidian, a green pine cone, a shark's tooth. I've still got the George the Sixth penny."

Jeff dropped a wonton back in the bowl. "The dead spider in the matchbox freaked me out."

"You remember that? You screamed your little head off. Poor Squidgy! Oh, I remember so much about those days! I thought Beck was the most important person in the world."

There was a silence and when Jeff looked up, he saw that her eyes were glassy with tears. He leaned towards her. "Mum and Dad will get over it, Andy. They're really happy about Sydney. They'll stop being so hard on Beck."

"Don't count on it," she said.

A waitress asked if they would like more jasmine tea. When she saw a trail of tears on Andrea's face, she looked awkward, lost for words, and turned away. Jeff gave his sister his spare paper serviette. She spread it across her face and blew her nose.

He looked away from the table to the window and the after-work crowd that flowed in two directions along the pavement. Only one person outside wasn't moving. He spotted her at once. The old woman again! Standing against a verandah post, and looking into the restaurant! The clothes were different, no hat this time, but it was impossible to mistake that face.

Jeff grabbed his sister's arm. "Over there!"

Andrea saw her too, but only for a second. More people blocked their view and when they had passed, the woman was gone. Jeff stood up to peer over the heads. "That was her, wasn't it? The old woman?"

Andrea didn't answer. She looked as though she couldn't believe what her eyes had taken in. Her face was as pale as the paper serviette in her hand,

and Jeff knew that behind her stillness, her thoughts were screaming.

* * *

While Andrea microwaved the food, Jeff started to set the table.

Winston and Helen were arguing about a packet of documents that were coming by courier. At least, that was how the row started.

"Why the hell didn't you have them sent to your office?" Helen snapped.

"I told them! Of course, I did! But Warren could have given him our home address. His lawyer hasn't been here. He wouldn't know a courier doesn't have access to this property. I needed you at home to release the gate —"

"If a courier had come, there'd be a notice in the mailbox." She turned her chair slightly to focus on the TV news, some big bomb blast in Afghanistan.

"You should be here!" He hit the table with his fist. "In this house! Isn't it good enough for you?"

"Oh, shut it, Wins." She grabbed the remote and turned up the sound.

He talked louder. "I come home at night, the kids are here, no mother, no dinner, packets of noodles and pizzas out of the freezer. Where are you? Selling tours in a travel agency!"

"Sometimes," she said, "I have to work late."

"You don't have to work at all!"

"So you keep saying, and I keep telling you: I — want — to — work!"

Winston grabbed the remote from her and switched off the kitchen TV. His voice was loud in the silence. "Work here — in your own home. I will pay you executive wages, twice your salary — three times —"

She took a deep breath. "I work to get away from this place!"

"If that's the problem, you can play golf. I'll get you a new set of clubs." He ran his hand over his head and became calmer. "I know a good coach. Helen, you'd enjoy getting involved. You already know at least half a dozen women who play down there."

"How many times must I tell you!" Helen yelled. "I like my job!"

It was Andrea who interrupted. She thrust a bowl of toasted cashew nuts between them and said, "If you two don't stop, Jeff and I are running away from home."

Neither parent thought that funny, but they stopped arguing. Winston stood up and tucked in his shirt as though he were getting himself together, while Helen grabbed a handful of cashews with one hand and the TV remote in the other, and went back to watching the evening news.

Winston said to Jeff, "Did you see a courier notice in the mailbox or under the gate?"

"No." Jeff laid the red chopsticks neatly next to the two place mats. "Something might come tomorrow."

Andrea placed two dishes of chicken rice on the table. "Jeff and I had ours in town. We brought this back for you."

"You went to town after school?" said Winston.

"That Chinese place near the library," said Jeff.

Winston turned to Helen. "You see? This is what I mean when I say this household is totally out of control. The children come home hungry and have to go out to get a meal."

"Fantastic, Dad," said Andrea. "What about – thank you for thinking of us, Andrea. That's very kind of you, Andrea."

"I'm on your side, here, girl," he said.

Helen stood up, switched off the TV, picked up her plate from the table and took it into her office.

Winston pulled a chair out from under the table and raised his eyebrows at Andrea and Jeff. "Your mother's having a bad day," he explained.

* * *

Andrea's bedroom was bigger than Jeff's, with space for two fat armchairs shaped like pouty lips. Bright red, too. They were cushy comfortable, although

Jeff sometimes had nightmares about being eaten by a greedy chair. Tonight they sat in the chairs with their homework, Andrea making notes for her sociology essay, Jeff using her iPad to research current environmental issues that influenced politics. Neither of them could concentrate.

Eventually, Andrea looked up. "Don't let them get to you."

"I don't."

"Yes, you do. You are turning in on yourself like an ingrown toenail."

He had to laugh, because he had one of those, a nail shaped like half a barrel, sides digging into the skin of his big toe.

"Beck couldn't stand it," she said. "I remember the rows. It's not just Dad. They are both heavily into control."

He was still smiling. "Remote control."

"You said it." She looked at him. "Hey! When you asked me if I was going to leave school, did you think I might go off somewhere and desert you?

He didn't answer.

"I would never do that," she said.

"People change," he said. "People always change."

"You are my squidgy little brother. I used to feed you in your high chair. I taught you to float and do belly flops. You used to say to me, 'I love you this much.'" She held out her arms.

He remembered them both doing belly flops at the city pool and how she stopped because she was getting lady bumps on her chest and they hurt when she hit the water face down.

"We still love each other this much." Her arms stayed stretched out. "And we love Beckett this much. We have to stick together, you, me, Beck. We just have to!"

There grew a warmth in him that melted the tension in his stomach. He nodded again and scrolled down to an article on the impact of mining on native fauna. After a while, he said, "Andy, that was her, wasn't it? Today? Outside the restaurant?"

Her hands became still on her keyboard, her eyes fixed on the screen. "Could have been," she said. "It did look a bit like her."

Her voice was too light. That was how he knew that she, too, thought the old woman was more than strange.

★ ★ ★

Mrs Wilson gave him eight out of ten for his project on New Zealand native snails threatened by a mining company. He would have preferred nine out of ten, but Paul got a nine – so that was the next best thing.

"Generally, there was some interesting creative

spelling," said Mrs Wilson. "Gentlemen, this was not meant to be your sloppy copy. In fact, if it were a job application, I'm afraid you'd all be unemployed and in the dole queue. Remember, we have the spelling competition next week, so I'm giving you a little extra homework this weekend."

There were groans around the room.

"I promise it won't kill you. You might even enjoy it." She looked around the room. "Where's Ludwig?"

Someone knew. "Fell off his bike and broke a bone."

"Oh. Poor Ludwig." Her face creased with sympathy. "Where is the fracture?"

They all looked to someone else, but no one had that information.

"If you fell off your bike and incurred a fracture, where would that be likely?" She ignored a few sniggers. "Come on boys, what do you remember about bones?"

"I might break a leg," volunteered Salosa.

"Your leg has three bones. Your foot has fifty-two bones. Where is the break? Anyone, tell me! Jeffrey?"

Jeff didn't want to answer. He would have said tibia or fibula but this was way off track, Mrs Wilson getting lost again, like a dog chasing a rabbit. She was supposed to be handing out the spelling sheets.

Paul said, "We don't know where Ludwig had the fracture."

"It's a hypothetical question, Paul. The human body has two hundred and sixty bones. Maybe you can name one."

Jeff raised his hand to shoulder height. "Mrs Wilson, a baby is born with two hundred and seventy bones."

She looked at him.

"It's true," he said. "Afterwards some of the bones fuse together, but, actually, babies are born perfect."

"That's an interesting statement," she said. "Tell us more, Jeffrey."

He couldn't. His face was hot and he clicked his ballpoint pen, in, out, in, out. Two and seven. In his numbers game, the skeleton of a newborn baby was a nine. How could he explain that?

★   ★   ★

When he arrived home, there was no one there but big Eddie, who had been planting spring bulbs along one wall and was now scooping some stray leaves out of the swimming pool. The sun was still high and Eddie's forehead had beads of sweat like transparent pimples. Jeff wondered why Eddie only did gardening when he was good at so many things, like making furniture and fixing cars.

"How are you, kid? How was the day at school?"

"Okay, I suppose." He needed to say something

more. "The pool looks nice. I mean, you keep it nice and clean."

"It's a waste. No one ever uses it."

"We use it. Sometimes. I had a swim two days before the storm."

Eddie shrugged and went down a step to pick something out of the water, a dark green beetle. He put it carefully on a stone in the cactus garden, then took up his net to scoop another leaf. "It's all a bit of a waste. Four families could live in this house, you know. Twenty kids could swim in the pool. Don't you ever feel it's a bit big for four people?"

"No."

Eddie nodded as though the answer needed a lot of thought, and Jeff immediately went into his room and changed into his bathing shorts. He came out, ran across the concrete and did a spectacular plunge into the pool.

Oh, it was cold. It was really cold. He stood gasping, and then did two vigorous lengths of crawl with Eddie watching.

"That's pretty good, man," said Eddie. "You got your arms and legs going fine in synch, but try not to bring your shoulders out of the water when you breathe."

Jeff wiped his face. "What do you mean?"

"Resistance. You lose speed. Keep your body straight and roll on the downstroke so your mouth is out. Look. Like this." He lay on the concrete at the edge of the pool, like a huge sea lion. "Roll like this. See? You keep your shoulders straight and you don't lose speed. Try it."

Jeff would have tried it, but at that moment Winston appeared through the glass doors, dark suit, briefcase in hand. "What's going on?"

Eddie got to his feet. "Afternoon, Mr Lorimer."

"He was showing me how to breathe." Jeff climbed out of the pool, hugging himself. "I lift my shoulders out of the water and it slows me down."

Winston walked up to Eddie, really close. "I don't pay you to be my son's swim coach. Jeff, go inside at once!"

Jeff ran past them, into the house, dripping on the cold marble floor. He turned on the shower and stood shivering under the hot water, his arms still clenched around his chest. What is a number? A multitude composed of units. What is a line? A length without a breadth. What is a square? A quadrilateral which is both equilateral and right-angled. He stopped shivering and rested his head against the shower wall. "I hate him," he said. "I hate him, I hate him."

* * *

The next morning, Saturday, he biked to the library to return some books. The place was crowded, elderly people fumbling with their cards and big print novels, mothers trying to stop toddlers from pulling books out of shelves, a man reading the newspapers, several people at the computers, a woman complaining about the price of coffee and another yelling at a child who was standing on a table. Jeff guessed there were as many words hanging in the air as there were trapped in pages. He handed in the books and was wondering if he should take more out, when he got that familiar sensation under his ears. Pressure. He turned quickly. Yes, she was standing in the narrow aisle between Philosophy and Psychology, in that dark padded jacket with the pink scarf and knitted hat, leaning forward, her hand folded over a wooden walking stick. She watched him with something like a smile. Her eyes were dark and unblinking.

His instinct told him to bolt out the door and not look back, but his feet did not move. His mind of its own accord started counting seconds. One, two, three, four …

She waited. He guessed she knew he wouldn't run away. He walked slowly towards her, weaving around people until he was close enough to see the thin cracks around her mouth.

"How are you, Jeff?" she said.

"Okay. How are you?"

"You want the truthful answer or a polite one?"

She thrust her head forward, her gaze full of mischief.

"Truth," he said.

"I wish I wasn't here. I hate this prison you call a body. The real Maisie was glad to be leaving it. You don't often see them so excited. Going home, she was, like a child running down a hill. She said I could use her body, only it was no gift, believe me. I had to take it. It's my job. Do you mind if I sit down?"

"No, no." He remembered his manners and pulled out a library chair with a padded seat. She sank down with a sigh, the stick between her knees, her hands folded over the top. Her hair was fluffy at the edges of the hat, floating against the purple wool, like cobweb. He dared to say, "What is your job?"

"I already I told you. I'm one of the dream-keepers."

He wondered if a dream-keeper was like a dream-catcher, a Native American weaving, round, with beads and feathers, an object that people hung above their beds so they would have pleasant dreams. Andy had a dream-catcher from a friend in America.

He smiled politely. "I don't dream a lot," he said.

"Number Nine, you live in a dream. You all do. What you call life is a dream and you don't wake up until you die. I'm in the dream now too, and I'd much rather be awake because this old body is more a nightmare, if you don't mind me saying so. I got stuck in the bath, this morning. The arms and legs wouldn't work to get me out."

"I don't understand," he said.

"What an old body has to do is turn over. You get on hands and knees and then stand, holding on to the edge of the bath so you don't slip. But I suppose by the time you're old, you'll have forgotten that bit of wisdom."

"I'm sorry. I mean I don't understand about living in a dream."

She tapped her stick on the carpet. "That's because you're too young to know where you are going, too old to remember where you came from. How can I make it clear? When your spirit inhabits a body, it goes into the dream you call life. Then all you know is the information that comes to you through the body's five senses, what you see, hear, taste, smell, touch. The rest is a forgetting."

"Forgetting?" He was puzzled.

"None of this will make much sense to you now, but try to remember my words. They'll mean survival when you need it. They're about something unchanging."

"You mean mathematics?" he said. "That's unchanging."

"Ah!" Her eyes glinted. "We'll get to numbers in a moment. This is the bit to remember. Your little dream of life exists between the sleep you call birth and the waking you call death. The bigger reality is all around you right now, but you are shut off from it by those limited senses."

"What bigger reality?" He glanced away and saw that people were watching. "Are you talking about the universe?"

"You're supposed to be smart! Not the universe as you know it. That's a product of your senses. The big reality! How do I explain it? I'm talking about the realm of spirit! A word that might have meaning for you is Light."

"Light?"

"Yes, Light." She smiled showing her broken teeth. "Look inside yourself, Jeff. You come from the Light and you still have a memory of the Light in you. Go deep and find it. Hold on to it. Sure as gravity, you'll need it in the changes. It will tell you what to do."

Changes. The word made his breath catch and he felt fear. He already knew there was going to be big change. He saw it coming like the great black cloud that marched before last week's storm.

She read his feelings. "Don't fuss, Number Nine. It's part of the paths you and your family have chosen and it's meant to be. The outcome will be right for all of you."

He stared at her. "You know about us. I don't even know your real name."

"Maisie will have to do," she said.

"Miss — Maisie, you were going to say something about mathematics."

"Was I?"

"Yes, you said —"

"Then I've forgotten." She waved her hand in front of her face. "It's an old brain. There are gaps between the synapses."

"The brain has one hundred billion cells," he reminded her.

"Not all of mine are in working order," she snapped. "One hundred thousand, one hundred billion — who cares? Numbers cross over into the larger reality, the same here as there. Now I'm tired. You'd better go." She shut her eyes in dismissal.

He stood for a few seconds but she didn't look at him again, so he took three steps backwards and left the library.

*　*　*

Walking up the hill towards home, Jeff paused to look down at the harbour. It was a great pond of light, water dancing with sun dazzle. Was that the kind of Light she meant? If it was, there was certainly no sparkle inside him. It was puzzling when you felt something had meaning but didn't know what that meaning was.

He arrived at the top of the hill and saw a man

standing at the intercom by their locked gate. He had grey hair, a grey moustache and he wore blue overalls, paint-stained, ragged at the knees.

"Who are you looking for?" Jeff asked.

"Mr or Mrs Lorimer," the man replied.

"There's no one home," Jeff said.

"That explains it then," the man said. "I've been pressing the bell for a good five minutes. Do you belong here?"

He nodded. "I'm their son, Jeff Lorimer."

The man held out his hand, "Pleased to meet you, Jeff. I'm Henry Sorensen, the replacement gardener."

5

EARTH'S CRUST varies in thickness, thinner under oceans and thicker under the continents. The inner core and the crust are solid. The outer core and mantle layers are plastic and semi-fluid. The crust extends from the surface down 40 km, and the upper mantle from 40 km to 400 km. There is a transition region, 400–650 km, before the lower mantle, which is 650–2700 km. The "D" layer, 2700–2890 km, surrounds the outer core, which is 2890–5150 km. The depth of the inner core is 5150–6378 km.

Each of the seven layers has distinct chemical and seismic properties.

Andrea wasn't home. She had promised to take him to a movie, but she had been gone all day. Winston was at his office, and Helen went to the supermarket before having a cappuccino with two old school friends. When she came in, she had the car to unpack, groceries to put away, and she was short with words.

"Eddie wasn't suitable," she said, stacking the frozen foods.

"He was. He knew everything about gardens. You tell me one thing he did that wasn't right."

"Don't argue, Jeffrey. I get enough of that from your sister. It was your father's decision, and he decided Mr Sorensen was more experienced."

"Experienced how?"

"He does landscape gardening. He's a professional. Will you stop sulking and take these through to the laundry?"

He carried two packets of laundry powder to the back of the house and stowed them in the laundry cupboard. Through the glass-panelled door he could see the cactus garden and a corner of the pool. He walked back to the kitchen, nineteen steps instead of the usual twenty-one. "Dad hated Eddie and it wasn't Eddie's fault."

His mother didn't look at him. "Nonsense," she said.

"It's true. Dad's homophobic."

Helen closed the fridge door. "Jeffrey! That's disgusting! Where do you get language like that? Would you be happy if I told your father what you just said?"

"You can! I don't care."

"Stop! Not one more word!" She put some

apples into the bowl on the counter. "I don't like your tone. You can go to your room."

"I can't. I've got cricket." Anger made him strong. He took an apple from the bowl, and bit into it hard, imagining that he had titanium teeth slicing through a cricket ball.

"No cricket!"

"Mum, I have to go to cricket. Mr Ingles said!"

"I will phone Mr Ingles and tell him you're gated," Helen said. "This is a family matter and more important than boys batting a ball around a playing field."

His anger increased, flaring into his hands, making them want to smash things, throw stuff across the room. He curled his fingers into fists and thrust them in his pockets. "We don't bat a ball around a field! This is cricket! If you came and watched some of our games, you'd know something about it."

"Jeffrey, one more word and you're gated next Saturday as well. I'm not telling you again. Go to your room." She pointed with a straight arm and finger that looked so ridiculous, he would have laughed if he hadn't been upset.

He went because there was nowhere else to go, and lay face down on the bed, his breath hot on the pillow. Why wasn't Andrea here? She had promised. The movies didn't matter. He could watch a film any time, anywhere. It was what she said about them sticking together. We are all we've got, she'd once told him. Was that only true for the moment of the saying?

His breathing became slower and the anger subsided into a feeling of helplessness and sadness. Eddie had gone. He rolled over onto his back and somewhere between himself and the ceiling, saw a picture of the gardener lifting that green beetle out of the swimming pool. It was such a clear memory, Eddie's smooth brown fingers cupped under the little thing, taking it to the cactus garden, and then tilting it so that it slid onto a dry flat stone, its legs waving. He'd turned it over. The green shell on its back separated like elevator doors and two little wings came out to carry it away to some place it knew to be home. Jeff blinked. The other memory was his father large in his dark office suit, shouting across the yard as he walked towards the gardener. Jeff had run into the house, leaving Eddie with Winston, and something had happened to make it Eddie's last day in the garden. What had his father said to Eddie? Was this what the woman had meant by change? He sat up and swung his legs over the side of the bed. The old lady, Maisie or whatever her name was, had told him there would be big changes, and he had felt something in him respond to that, something like an electric shock in his body.

It was hard to know what was real with that old lady. Most of the time, she seemed to be wandering around some dark maze in her brain, where sentences deconstructed and then glued together again in random ways. Helen's great-aunt was like that. She stared at you with vacant eyes and just as you got to thinking that all the rungs had fallen off her ladder, she turned on you and asked you the score of last night's rugby test match. But Maisie was a bit different. Great-aunt Rose said mostly nonsense and some things that were real. The Maisie lady had three categories: nonsense, real, and other statements that weren't logical but had an effect on him, like they were something he was supposed to know but had forgotten.

He wanted to talk to Andrea about the conversation in the library.

It was very important that he do that. He tried again to phone her, but of course her mobile was switched off and there was no point in leaving a message. Instead he sent her a text message: *Did u no E was fired? J.*

Afterwards, he realised that of course Andrea would know. She was up to date with everything that happened in the family. Besides, he didn't want to talk about Eddie as much as about the old gum tree woman who was attaching herself to him for some reason. If he was to find out why, he needed to know more about her, and that meant separating the real from the craziness. Maybe a good way to start would be to find out more about dementia. He sat at his desk and started his computer. It had barely booted up when there was a soft knock on the door and Helen came in.

"You can go to cricket," she said.

He swivelled in his chair. That meant she had probably phoned Mr Ingles, who had left her in no doubt that he wanted all the team at the clubhouse at one o'clock. He wanted to say, I told you so, but couldn't risk as much as a smile. She was still angry with him.

She came into the room and sat on the edge of the bed. "Jeffrey, parents are not as stupid as children believe. I know what it's like to be your age. You don't know what it's like to be mine."

He didn't answer.

"Your father did what he thought was right, and I agreed with his decision. It was our decision to make – not yours, not the gardener's. I want you to understand that."

"I understand," he said. "Is that it?"

"No." She folded her hands in her lap. "There is something else. I need to tell you that Beckett is coming back to New Zealand next month. He'll be in prison in Auckland. We haven't been given the exact date of his transfer but I think we can be sure it will all be very public again – newspapers, television."

"Aren't you pleased he's coming back?"

"Well, of course, we're pleased. He's much safer over here. But you may wish to be prepared for questions. People will know, although, thank God, not everyone will connect the name with us. There are a surprising number of Lorimers."

He waited.

"Jeffrey, if someone asks you, you won't be telling a lie if you say he is not a part of our family."

"But he is! Mum, he's my brother!"

"Sweetie, we gave Beckett every chance and he betrayed us time and time again. Your father even believed him when he claimed he was framed. That was just another lie. The cocaine wasn't in his suitcase, it was strapped around his middle. But it started long before that, one disappointment after another. Criminal friends. Unpaid fines. Arrested for being drunk and disorderly. I believe that a family has the right to divorce an ungrateful child, so I'm saying, you won't be telling a lie –"

Andrea's words echoed in his head, don't let them get to you, and then, for some odd reason, he remembered the feeling of Beck's hand in his when he was four and scared of balloons. He stood up. "I need to go," he said. "Mr Ingles will be waiting for the team."

* * *

That night he told Andrea about the meeting with the woman in the library. She was sorting the clothes in her wardrobe, and she listened but in a dreamy sort of way. At one stage, she asked, "Did you feel scared?"

He thought about that. "Not really."

"She's a strange old thing. If you feel threatened, you should tell someone."

"I don't feel threatened, and I'm telling you."

Andy rattled coathangers. "You know what I mean, Squidge. If she's following you, you should say something to Mum or Dad."

He felt hurt by the way she had offloaded a confidential matter and he changed the subject. "I thought we were going to a movie today."

"And I thought you were playing cricket."

"Not all day, Andy."

"Some other time, eh? Sorry, Squidge, I've got a lot of things on my mind. Yeah, we'll do a movie. Promise. And I'm sorry about Eddie getting the push. I know you liked him."

He nodded.

She put her hand over his. "He'll get another job, and it will be better than this one. I mean, how would you like to work for Dad?"

He looked up at her and his smile met the laughter in her eyes. "I wouldn't. But I had this idea –" He looked down again. "It seemed like I was the cause somehow. Dad told me not to talk to him, and I did."

"No, no, no." She shook her head. "It's not you. It's the way Dad's mind works. He is so ignorant. Eddie is gay. He's not a paedophile. Don't worry, Squidge. The sacking of Eddie has nothing to do with you."

"I hate it when bad things happen," he said.

She didn't answer, but she sat beside him for more than a minute, before getting up. "Have to go," she said. "I've got homework."

But when he passed her room a few minutes later, he saw she had on her headphones and was watching music videos on her computer. She wanted to be alone.

★ ★ ★

Everyone was quiet over dinner. Helen had cooked a meal, spaghetti bolognaise, and had defrosted an apple cake with a cinnamon crust.

Jeff was the only one who said it tasted good. Winston didn't even ask him about the cricket. Andrea pushed her plate away, food half eaten, and went to her room. It was early evening and dusk seemed to bring a great emptiness as the sun dragged the light towards the other side of the world.

Light, Maisie said. Light had meaning for him. But what meaning?

After dessert, Winston pushed back from the table,

screeching the chair on the polished marble. He said to Helen, "I'm on that early flight Monday."

"Are you coming back the same day?" she asked.

"Yes. I'll leave the car at the airport. Excuse me." He stood, pushed the chair back in, and went down the hall to his office.

As Helen stacked the plates, she glanced at Jeff. "Sydney," she said.

"Is something wrong?" he asked.

"No. Nothing. There has been a little hold-up in the registration of the title deeds, and the quickest way to sort it is to be on the spot."

"What's wrong with phone and emails?"

Helen smiled. "You know your father. He likes to be hands-on, and I have no doubt that he wants to gloat over his Sydney property. I'm sure he'll have the new house keys in his pocket before he leaves."

Andrea came through to help with the dishes. As she stacked the plates, Helen put a hand out to stop her. "I'll do these. Why don't you two go into the theatre and watch one of your father's DVDs?"

Jeff leaned towards Andrea, doing please, please, in sign language.

She laughed, nodded a yes, and they went into the theatre next to Winston's office.

They had seen all the videos in the collection, but Jeff was allowed to choose and he pounced on *Inception* because it was one of his favourites – that and *The Matrix*. He'd already seen *Inception* three times and with each viewing it had revealed more to him, making the incredible credible. He loved the way people could go through layers of experience in the brain, descend one level after another and then come up again to external reality. But he seriously doubted they could do that in real life.

They had to keep the sound down because Winston was working next door. That was okay. They both knew the dialogue. They sprawled in adjacent leather chairs and Andrea put her arm over his shoulders. He rested his head against her and watched the film, her hair against his cheek. He wanted to stay that way forever.

★   ★   ★

Some days after school, Jeff went to the Argonaut Travel Agency to get a ride to the house with Helen. One of those days was Monday. The girls in the office knew him and took no notice when he found a chair and a magazine. He was a part of the place. However, the man and woman waiting next to him asked him where he was planning to travel.

"Home," he said, and then he pointed with his thumb. "That's my mother."

He was proud of Helen at her work. She always looked elegant and she smiled a lot at customers, which made her eyes crinkle and shine. Behind her was a large poster of the Parthenon in Athens, white against a blue sky. He had seen it many times and knew it by its statistics, finished in 438 BC, sixty-nine and a half metres long and almost thirty-one metres wide. There were other, smaller scenes around the room: buildings less old, snow-capped mountains, white ships on blue oceans, no rain or grey skies to be seen. People said that photos did not lie, but that was not true. Photos lied all the time. Like movies, they could be mostly make-believe.

The couple in the seats next to him went to the agent near his mother. Helen was putting tickets and information in a travel wallet for the man sitting by her desk. She stood to shake his hand and then, as the man walked past Jeff and out the door, she turned off her computer.

Her smile was gone and she was Mum again, shrugging on her jacket and shaking the car keys at Jeff. He followed her out to the car park behind the building and waited while she unlocked the Audi. "Have you heard from Dad?" he asked.

"He phoned."

He sank into the passenger seat and pushed his backpack in front of his feet. "I don't want to live in Sydney."

"We're not. Who said we were?" She adjusted the rear vision mirror and backed out of the park.

He turned to face her. "Isn't that why he went over today?"

"No. It's something else."

"Like what?"

"Nothing major. A small hiccup in the paperwork." She swung the wheel and the car nosed into the traffic. "He'll have it sorted by now."

"When does he get back?"

"Late. We won't wait up. We'll get takeaways tonight and you can choose. What's it to be – Chinese, Thai, curry? You like rogan josh, don't you?"

He didn't answer. When she said Thai, his thinking had flipped to Beckett coming back from Thailand and he remembered how he was supposed to tell people that his brother was not a part of their family.

Had they forgotten Beck's laughter, all the tricks? Like the time he answered the phone, saying, "Good evening, this is the morgue," and when he got Andy to burst a paper bag that had flour in it. How many times had their mother said, "Oh Beckett!" and flicked him with a tea towel? Had they forgotten who he was? Dad had been so proud of Beck. "My son's getting a commerce degree," he'd say, as though a BCom. was something extraordinary. Then Beck dropped out of uni, and the rows began, one after another.

"Let's settle for rogan josh and mango lassi," said Helen.

He nodded. Helen was a salesperson. She was like the posters in the Argonaut office that told lies by leaving out the truth. It's what they needed to do to make people buy what they had to offer.

∗ ∗ ∗

That night he looked up dementia and found that the old meaning of the word was "out of mind" – de-mentia. The most common form was Alzheimer's, although people could get dementia at any age from brain injury, infection, strokes, loss of blood to the brain.

He went through the long list of symptoms and saw in them Helen's Great-aunt Rose with her long wispy hair and doll-like eyes. She had memory loss, and couldn't solve problems or do familiar tasks. She got confused about time and place and she thought the hospital was her old school. When she saw herself in a mirror, she was convinced she had a visitor. It was difficult for Great-aunt Rose to follow conversations. She kept misplacing things – like her glasses, which were on a cord around her neck but she took them off and put them in the fridge because they were a necklace from the Queen and needed to go into the bank for safe keeping. The more he read, the more he remembered the times he had visited her. He saw those pale empty eyes, the crooked lipstick, and the way her mouth trembled when she pointed at him and said, "Are you the doctor's boy?"

He went from one article to another, but it was all about his faded relative who had once been a talented music teacher and singer. There was nothing he could connect with the Maisie woman.

The old woman who had come into his life had a different kind of craziness, and because he didn't know what that was called, he couldn't access information about it. Words like the names of foreign foods came up on the dementia sites – schizophrenia, paranoia, bipolar, Alzheimer's again. They were all conditions tucked away in the brain, listed with their symptoms and their treatments. None of those were Maisie.

It was late when he put his light out. It seemed he had been asleep only minutes when he heard his father's voice in the kitchen. He was home and they were having one of their arguments, Winston's words rising in waves of sound, Helen's a persistent current, pushing, pushing. He didn't know what it was about but guessed that his father was going to make them all move to Sydney to get away from the publicity of Beckett returning to New Zealand.

A desperate thought came into his head. He didn't mean it, but said it anyway, out loud and into the pillow. "I'd rather kill myself."

SOUND *is a sequence of waves of pressure through a medium such as air or water, and the perception of sound is limited to a certain range of frequencies. For humans, hearing is normally between the frequencies of 20 Hz and 20 000 Hz, although the upper limit often decreases with age. Other species have different ranges of hearing and many species have produced special organs to generate sound. Sound cannot travel through a vacuum.*

They were not moving to Sydney. The argument was about something else, Jeff didn't know what, that had put his father into a state of major irritation.

Although Winston had come home late, he was up early and pacing about the kitchen, phoning, checking emails, shouting at Helen for no reason. He couldn't sit down for more than a few seconds.

His arms moved, his legs twitched, as though someone was pulling strings.

"Have you got hold of him?" Helen said, as she put out the breakfast cereals.

"I can't! I told you! His health won't take long flights. He's going back in short hops, Darwin, Singapore, Hong Kong, Rome, Berlin, London. Rest days in between."

"Surely he can answer his phone," Helen said.

"His bloody phone's off!" Winston threw up his hands. "If you can't say anything intelligent, just shut the hell up!"

Helen's mouth went thin and her movements slowed. She put bowls deliberately in place, a glass of orange juice beside each, and told Jeff to go and wake up his sister.

Andrea was already up and dressed but she looked half asleep, hair all over her face and dark marks under her eyes. She, too, was grumpy. "I've been sleeping in a war zone."

"It's Sydney. Something's gone wrong."

"Who cares?" She picked up her hairbrush. "Listen to him! I don't know how any of us put up with his moods."

"Breakfast is ready," he said.

"I'm not hungry."

"You'll be late for school."

"Too bad!"

"Andy, you have to come for breakfast!"

"Oh, go away! You're as bad as he is! Control, control!" She looked at him in the mirror and her expression changed. She jumped up and gave him a clumsy hug. "I didn't mean it, little bro."

He shrugged within the squeeze of her arms. "I know."

"You'll never be like him. Never! All right, I'll come out and have some orange juice."

* * *

It was Mrs Wilson's birthday, although she wouldn't say how old she was. Paul reminded the class that a lady never told her age, and Mrs Wilson said it wasn't that, she had just given up counting when she got to a hundred. This made them laugh, everyone except Clive Fisher, who didn't get the joke and remarked that she had to be exaggerating.

They had put money together to buy her a ball-point pen with a rolled-gold cap and her name on the barrel. Salosa's father had a shop that did engraving, but because they were unsure of her first name, the pen simply had *Mrs Wilson* on it, which was appropriate for a school pen. They had all signed the card and Peter had written that the pen was designed to give high marks to pupils' assignments.

They were right in assuming Mrs Wilson would be

so pleased, she would fritter away a good percentage of a history lesson. "Do you know, when my mother was at school, the desks had holes for little pots of ink they called inkwells and students had to use pens with nibs that were dipped in the ink."

They knew how to keep her stories going. Salosa said, "When were ball-point pens invented, Mrs Wilson?"

"Some time in the forties, I think," she said. "But students were not allowed to use them. Teachers thought it would make their script sloppy. Ballpoint pens would ruin handwriting! That was the catchphrase of the day."

"What about smart phones?" someone said.

Mrs Wilson chuckled. "I'll leave you to answer that. Have you all got your history text? Turn to page seventy-three —"

Peter quickly put up his hand. "Is it true, Mrs Wilson, that ball-point pens don't write in outer space?"

"Correct, Peter!" she said. "The first astronauts discovered their ball-point pens would not work in zero gravity. So, do you know what happened?"

They all did, because she had told this story before.

"NASA scientists spent ten years and billions of dollars designing a ball-point pen that would write in any condition, upside down, under water, in zero gravity, in all temperatures and on any surface, including glass."

They waited for the punchline.

"And do you know what the Russians did? They used a pencil!"

Everyone else laughed as expected, but Jeff merely shook his head. It was not a funny story. It was a comment on the evolution of the human race.

* * *

After school, Paul invited Jeff to come around and have a jam session in the basement. Jeff wanted to say yes, but couldn't with the way things were at home. All day he had carried his father's angry voice and while he wanted to get as far away from that as possible, he also needed to find out what was going on. He said, thanks, another day, to Paul, and then walked to Argonaut Travel.

Tuesdays, he usually took the bus home because Helen worked late, but today he didn't want to go back to a house that echoed bad energy. Then there was the other thing, a stranger doing Eddie's work in the garden. So much change! Even if his mother was working late today, she could spare a minute to tell him what was happening.

Because it was a fine afternoon, he walked along the wharf. At least, that was the reason he gave himself. Actually, he was hoping to see Maisie somewhere in that public space. All along the waterfront were seats where old people often sat, watching boats and enjoying the sunshine. It was a logical setting. Maybe she would be there.

He strolled past the three red tugboats snuggled up against the pier, past the *Dominion Post* ferry, past the restaurants, his head turning. There was a party of Asian tourists taking photos, a couple on a tandem bicycle, children, parents, some kids with rollerblades. No old Maisie. He got as far as Circa Theatre and went right, leaving the sea to walk into the city and his mother's workplace. His sensible self asked him, how would Maisie know that he had decided to walk along the wharf? The answer was, the same way she knew he was going to be at the bus stop, the restaurant, the library.

Oh yeah? the voice argued. And how did she know that?

This time, the answer was silence.

By the time he arrived at the door of Argonaut Travel, he had walked two thousand, three hundred and twenty-seven steps.

There was a young redheaded woman sitting at Helen's desk. She smiled. "Are you Jeffrey? Hi! I'm Amiria. I'm filling in for your mother. She went home at lunchtime. She had a migraine."

Helen with a migraine? That was a headache, wasn't it? He stepped backwards. "Thanks."

"I used to get terrible migraines. Tell her putting

her head under a cold shower really helps. Hope she's better tomorrow."

★ ★ ★

Helen was home, cleaning the fridge. Winston was at the office. Outside, the grey-headed man with a moustache was clipping the small box hedge that separated the herb garden from the roses.

"It's a mess," Helen said. "Your father's trying to sort it out."

Jeff poured himself a chocolate milk. "What kind of mess?"

"I'm not sure. Neither is your dad. He's trying to get to the bottom of it, but it's possible we don't have that harbour property."

"The sale's fallen through?" He sat up straight, trying to conceal his pleasure. "So there's no Sydney house?"

Helen took the chocolate milk packet and put it back in the fridge. "It rather looks like it. No house. No courier package."

Jeff swallowed. The drink tasted wonderful. "No wonder Dad's upset."

"It's not the end of the world. He'll invest the money elsewhere."

She shut the fridge door. "At the moment he's talking about suing Mr Staunton-Jones's lawyer, so that's keeping him occupied. You've got chocolate milk down your shirt."

"I'm pleased," he said.

"What about?"

"About Sydney. I'm really, really glad."

"Your father had better not hear you saying that," she warned.

"Andy, too. We said we'd never move away from Wellington."

"There was never any question of moving."

"But it might have happened," he said. "Mr Staunton-Jones thought we were all going to live there. He talked about that."

"It was an investment. Nothing more. And it's not our only concern." Helen sat at the counter opposite him. She leaned forward. "Jeffrey, I know you and Andrea talk – about a lot of things. Does she ever say anything about Daniel?"

He knew where this was going. He shrugged. "Sometimes."

"Daniel thinks she's always busy with school work."

Jeff put his hands around his glass and felt the chill in his fingers. "She is busy with school work. If she's going to do law next year, she's got to get good marks. She works all hours."

"Nonsense," said his mother. "She's out all hours – and it's not with Daniel. Do you know who she's seeing?"

It was a relief to shake his head and mean it.

Helen watched him for a few seconds, then she got off the chair. "If you did know, you would tell me, wouldn't you?"

He tried a small smile. It worked. She put her hand on her forehead and said, "At least there is one person in this family I can rely on."

★   ★   ★

The historical figure Jeff had chosen for Mrs Wilson's assignment was Dmitri Mendeleev, who had created the periodic table. For Jeff, the man was not as important as the work that gave order to the world. The periodic table was like a holy book for scientists.

The computer gave a few statistics: Mendeleev was born in Siberia in 1834, and he died in 1907. There was a photograph, too, of an elderly bearded man at a desk. Jeff imagined him floating upside down in a space capsule, writing out the periodic table with a pencil, arranging the 65 elements he knew, in a grid. The elements were all neatly assembled according to ascending atomic weight.

It didn't matter to Jeff that the table was constructed from false reasoning. Electrons hadn't been discovered in Mendeleev's time. People thought the atom was the smallest particle. It took a whole forty-four years for them to discover the missing elements and work out the correct explanation. But it was Mendeleev who first knew that chemistry was simply numbers. Jeff wrote all that on his pad and then put down his pen. He picked up a 2B pencil and added, *The universe is made of numbers.*

★ ★ ★

It was dark and neither Winston nor Andrea was home. Helen and Jeff shared a microwaved lasagne, without conversation, Helen reading travel magazines while she ate. The house was so quiet that when the phone rang, they both jumped.

It was Paul Fitzgibbon, eager to talk to Jeff. "Hey, man, I'm in a sweat with the maths I didn't do yesterday. Fractions, okay. Percentages, okay. But what's with identifying linear functions? And this graphing of a proportional relationship? Did you do that?"

Jeff could almost see Paul tugging at his scruffy hair, something he always did when anxious. "Yes. They're not difficult."

"Can you come over, man? Dad can come and get you and if you like you can stay the night. Would you be cool with that?"

Words such as *saved*, *rescue*, *escape*, came into

his head and he didn't have to consider for long. "I think so. I'll need to ask Mum." He saw Helen looking at him, and added. "Here, you ask her."

She was careful, wanting to speak to Paul's parents, but in end she agreed and said he could go to school with Paul tomorrow. He ran, sixteen bounding steps, to his room and packed pyjamas, clean shirt and underwear, books.

Winston would be home soon and it would all start again. Andrea would walk in on it. "Sorry, Andy," he said to her empty room; but he wasn't sorry enough to stay. He went out the front door, ran along the drive, and waited outside the gate for Mr Fitzgibbon.

* * *

Paul's house was always noisy. Four-year-old Isabella had been to a library party and had her face painted like a tiger. She was now yelling because she didn't want it washed off, and her older sister was yelling that she'd mess up the pillow. Mrs Fitzgibbon came between them and said she'd rather wash a pillowcase than put up with the argument, so that was that. Jeff thought that Mrs Fitzgibbon came from Peru or Bolivia. She was a short woman with long black hair and a round face, and she often swore at the children in Spanish.

The noise in the Fitzgibbon house had a good feeling to it, like the noise in a farmyard. But it was hard to find a quiet corner of the kitchen table where Jeff could help Paul with his maths homework. It didn't take long. Paul was smart and once he understood the questions, he was finished in less than twenty minutes. He shoved the papers into his satchel and they were off to the basement for a session on keyboard and drums.

At eight-thirty, Mr Fitzgibbon came down to tell them supper was ready. A light meal at bedtime was usual in Paul's family. Jeff's mother said that one should not eat before going to sleep because the energy needed to digest food caused restlessness and bad dreams. Mrs Fitzgibbon had the opposite view. Food calmed the body, she said. A full stomach was a happy stomach that dreamed of heaven.

Whatever, her suppers were always good. Tonight it was grilled cheese and tomato on toast, which would sit well in lasagne. They sat around the table, Jeff and six Fitzgibbons, and the dog under the table like a furry vacuum cleaner. Jeff wished he could have a dog like that. He fed it bits under the table and let it lick his fingers.

Out of the blue, Paul's father said, "You must be pleased about your brother coming home."

Jeff went still. "What?"

"Beckett coming back to Auckland. I think the

government did a good job of negotiation. It'll be a relief for you all to have him here, safe and sound."

Paul, seeing Jeff's blank look, added, "It was on the six o'clock news."

"Was it?" Jeff put the toast down on his plate. "Did they say when?"

"Soon, they said." Mr Fitzgibbon looked at his wife. "Did they give a date?"

"I did not hear." She said to Jeff. "Your mama and your papa will be very happy. *La familia es todo.*"

"Family is everything," Paul translated.

Jeff's smile began inside him and spread out to his mouth and then to the faces around the table. He had not seen Beck for three years, two months and five days, and in every day of that time, he'd thought of him.

Now it was official. His brother was coming back. Winston would have seen the news. Helen too, and Andrea. At that moment, Jeff wanted to hug the entire Fitzgibbon family, even the sulky ex-tiger. "You're right," he said. "Everything."

7

LIGHT is an electromagnetic wave. The speed of light in a vacuum is commonly denoted c, the letter coming from celeritas, Latin for swiftness. It is a universal constant. Its value is 299,792,458 metres per second. Sunlight takes 8 minutes and 20 seconds to reach Earth, and 100,000 years to cross the Milky Way.

The news about Beckett was in the papers the next morning, and while Jeff was still at the Fitzgibbons, some people from TV had been to the house to interview Winston and Helen, who had refused to open the gates.

"We have nothing to say!" Winston had bellowed through the bars. "Nothing! The person you mention is not a part of this family!"

Jeff heard this from Andrea when he came home from school, and he saw that she'd been crying.

He looked around her room. It was a mess, drawers turned out, bed unmade. Her favourite T-shirt, with the slogan *Save Plankton, Kill Whales*, was on the floor with her netball gear. "You didn't go to college today," he said.

"No. I couldn't." She sat on the bed. "I'm so glad you weren't here, Squidge. It was terrible. Not just Dad. Mum, too. When the news came on, I said I was going to Auckland to see him, and they exploded. I reminded them I wasn't a little kid any more." She wiped her face on the corner of her bedsheet. "Mum said I was living in their house and they were paying expensive school fees. I had to do as I was told. It just kept getting worse. Then Dad said if I went to visit Beck, I was no longer welcome under his roof."

Jeff sat down beside her. His heart was thudding and he hardly dared breathe. "What are you going to do?"

She put her hand over his. "I'm sorry, Squidgy, I have to go. I just have to leave. I intended to go flatting next year, anyway, and I've decided to make the move now. Everything has changed. But I'll still see you."

He was so afraid, he could not say a word. She was going. He saw two suitcases behind the door. She was leaving him on his own.

"It's a flat in Thorndon," she said. "A friend rents it. His name is Mark."

Jeff pulled his hand away. "Don't tell me the name of your boyfriend!" he said. "They'll ask me!"

She stared at him. "How did you know?"

"I just knew." He looked at her. "Is he at school – or university?"

She made a noise that was half a laugh. "Mark is thirty-two."

He didn't say anything. Letters and numbers added and reduced in his head. The name was seven and the age was five.

"Little brother, I won't be far from here. I'll see you every day. Promise. I'll text you. I'll meet you after school and we'll go to the chocolate shop. We'll have burgers at McDonald's and I'll bring you letters from Beck."

He glanced again at the suitcases. "When are you leaving?"

"Today. Now. Before they get home. You'll be all right, Jeff. They like you. You're the good child."

"They like you too," he said.

"Only if I obey orders. But I'm like Beck was when he left home. I have to get away. I have to be me! I suppose I'll get a job. Please, please, understand I'm not deserting you."

He wanted to ask her what happened about sticking together, what about school and her plans for a law degree, but his throat was dry and his voice seemed to have retreated far inside his chest.

Andrea stood up and put some make-up stuff in a soft bag. "Have you seen the old lady again?" she asked.

He shook his head.

"I told Mum about her."

"Andy!"

"Just Mum. Not Dad. Squidge, I needed to say something. I'm not superstitious, but there's something strange about that woman. I'd even say sinister. Think of what's happened to this family since we found her under the tree. Dad gets caught up in a property scam, Eddie gets fired, Beckett's coming back from Thailand, I leave home. If this was the Middle Ages, I'd think she was some kind of witch."

But Jeff's thoughts had stopped at the first example. "What property scam?"

"Don't you know? It looks as though Mr Staunton marvellous Jones pulled a fast one, and Dad mightn't get his money back. They didn't tell me all the details, but this afternoon Dad gave a statement to the police."

"No!" He couldn't believe it. Not the man with the silver hair and smart grey suit who had been so kind and friendly! Surely, not that man! "What's going to happen?"

She shrugged. "When you find out, you can tell me. Will you give me a hand to get these to the car? Thanks, Squidge. I need to go before they are home."

* * *

Their argument with Andrea must have been big, because neither parent seemed surprised that she had gone. Winston, sitting on the sofa with his iPad, said, "She'll be back in a week, you mark my words." Then he went back to looking at emails.

Helen said, "I suppose she's moved in with a boyfriend."

"No, not a boy." Jeff turned away so he didn't have to look at his mother. "He's a man. His name is Mark."

"Mark who? Where does he live?"

"I don't know."

"You must know something. What does he do?"

"I told you, I don't know!" He was shouting.

"Bloody hell!" Winston got up, carrying his iPad. "Doesn't anyone in this house have an ounce of consideration? It would be nice if just one of you appreciated the situation we're in." His face was rcd. "We are in it because I've been working my arse off for this ungrateful family!" He glared at Helen and marched towards his office.

Helen called after him, "Well, I just hope to God she doesn't get pregnant. That's all we need!"

Jeff said quickly, "I've got homework to do."

But it wasn't that easy. Helen followed him to his room, and stood filling the doorway. "I thought you were the one person in this house I could trust."

He didn't answer. His computer hummed as he switched it on.

"Today I learned something else. That homeless woman who came the night of the storm – you've been seeing her."

"She's not homeless," he muttered. "She lives in some kind of pensioner apartment."

"Where?"

"I don't know."

"For a bright boy you don't know much, do you, Jeffrey? Why didn't you tell me she's been following you?"

He tried to look indignant. "She hasn't been following me! I saw her at the library."

Helen didn't move. "And the other times? There were other times, weren't there? What did she say to you?"

It was no good dodging the questions. Andrea had told her. He turned. "She wanted to thank me for the cushion and blanket I got her. You know, when she was lying by the tree."

"What else?"

"That was the only thing that made any sense." In a way, this was the truth. "She rambled a bit. She's old, she's got dementia like Great-aunt Rose."

"If you see her again, you will tell me." Helen was shaking her finger at him. "Understand?"

"Sure," he said.

"And if you find out Andrea's address, you will tell me that too." She turned to go, then looked back. "I can't tell you how much it hurts me that all three of my children are programmed for deceit."

For a long time, Jeff stared at his computer, which still had a photo of Dmitri Mendeleev on the screen. The old woman's words filled his mind. Winston, quicksand! Helen on a precipice! Andrea leaving school! You will know these things when you are ready for them, Maisie had said. Or similar words.

Dmitri Mendeleev, dead for more than a hundred years, stared back with the look of a man who was not comfortable with having his photograph taken. Jeff reminded him, "There is more to the universe than numbers." Then he wondered why he had said it. It was true, but he didn't know the truth until he'd heard it in his own voice.

* * *

That evening Helen asked him for his phone. At first, he thought it was being confiscated, then he realised she wanted to check his messages. He didn't mind that. He'd deleted all his old messages and there was a just a question from Clive about cricket next Saturday. Helen looked at it for a long time, and then handed the phone back without a word. That's when Jeff saw the new message, Andrea telling him that she had phoned her school about leaving, and she was going there tomorrow to pick up her books. The message finished with *LUS* for "love you Squidge", but she said nothing about Mark or their address, which made it okay because he didn't want to know that information.

He had no way of guessing that Helen would go to Andrea's school the next morning to collect her daughter's books and gym gear, and that she would find, between the pages of a media studies book, sheets of brown paper filled with pencilled writing – Beckett's letters.

* * *

The two men who came to the house did not look like detectives. One had a fat face and ears like paddles. The other was tall and very thin and he wore a yellow shirt with orange pineapples on it. As the tall one sat in an armchair opposite Winston and Helen, he said, "The boy should stay. He may have observed something that you or Mrs Lorimer missed."

He looked at his notes. "There is a daughter, too. Andrea. Is she here?"

"She's on holiday," said Helen. "Staying with a friend."

Winston invited them into his office, but they preferred to sit in the lounge around the coffee table.

"Spectacular view of the harbour," said the detective with the big ears. "All those yachts and ferries at your feet. You're on top of the world."

"I don't feel it!" Winston growled.

"You have my sympathy, Mr Lorimer," he replied. "If it's any consolation, and I'm sure it isn't, you're not the only one who's become a favourite adopted son of Julius Clarke, alias Warren Staunton-Jones, alias Carter McPherson, alias Sir Richard Walgrave. He cast a wide net with this Sydney scam. He caught six: two in Singapore, one in New Zealand and the rest in Australia, a total of nine million dollars."

"He was so sincere!" Helen said.

The tall detective folded himself into a chair. "He's very good at what he does, chooses the property carefully, chooses his victims. May I ask how you first met him, Mr Lorimer?"

"I told the officer. It was at an accountants' conference in Brisbane. He wasn't at the conference, just staying in the Marriott. We met in the bar."

"Ah yes. He took an instant liking to you and invited you to some place very prestigious and expensive. What was it? Box seats at the opera? A ride in his personal chopper to an offshore restaurant?"

Winston gave a short, sharp shake of the head and said, "The Royal Sydney Golf Club."

The plump detective pointed his pen at Winston. "This fellow is a professional. He takes time to groom his victims. He rents a property, forges the paperwork, dots all the i's and crosses the t's. How long did you know him?"

"I've already said all this. Do I have to go through it again?"

"Yes, sir, if you don't mind."

"Seventeen months," said Winston.

"And you say he flew to Wellington from Sydney to bring you the final documentation and the keys to the house. When was that again, sir?"

"Monday March eleven, the day after the storm."

"And that was the day you transferred the money, in total, one and a half million Australian dollars."

"Not to him!" Winston leaned forward. "It went to the lawyer, Vincent Pritchard, who was holding it in a special account until the title came through."

"Did you meet this Mr Pritchard?" asked the thin detective.

Winston hesitated. "No. I didn't think I needed to meet him. I knew him to be a senior partner in one of the most prestigious law firms in Sydney."

"According to his letterhead," said the plump man.

Winston sank back in the seat and briefly closed his eyes. "When I went to the firm, they'd never heard of Vincent Pritchard."

"So that was just another alias?" said Helen. "Mr Staunton-Jones' lawyer was really —"

The plump detective nodded.

"He seemed so genuine." Helen was holding back tears. "Do you know what he kept saying to my husband?"

"That your husband was the son he had never had? Yes. He used that line many times. I'm sorry. I know this is distressing for you."

Jeff leaned forward. "He said he wanted me for his grandson!"

The detective nodded. "This is not the movies, son. In real life people don't always look bad. Some of them look like angels."

Winston crossed and uncrossed his legs. "Look, fair's fair. We've given you all the information. Now we would like some answers. Where is this – this criminal right now? We live in the cyber world. There will be records of flights, bank transactions. If he's been working this racket for years, why hasn't he been arrested? I mean, what the hell is wrong with Interpol? I have to get my money back!"

The thin one said, "You can be sure the money has gone through several bank accounts by now, and that Julius Clarke has several passports."

"That's no excuse for not catching him!"

"Mr Lorimer, sir." The plump man was no longer smiling. "You wanted to buy a very desirable property that was, in fact, in a trust set up by an old Sydney family. Julius Clarke had short-term rental of this property. Sir, you are an accountant with Horton Fledger and Partners. You are a man naturally cautious with money. When he offered to sell it to you, what checks did you do?"

Helen cut in. "We trusted him!"

Winston added, "He sent it all by email, the title, history of previous ownership, original land claim, amenities map, ratings values. I suppose you'll tell us now they were all forgeries."

There was a long silence, and then the plump one said, "Sir, you know what they say. If something seems too good to be true, it probably is."

★ ★ ★

When the detectives left, Winston sat in one of the wooden deckchairs facing the harbour, and drank his whisky. The sun had set and the long shadows of potted plants had blurred and spread a cool greyness over everything on the patio.

Jeff stood inside the glass doors and watched his father, who was so still he could have been a statue except for the arm that held the glass. At this moment, some of the things Jeff had thought about his dad seemed unimportant. All the yelling and swearing that had driven Jeff into his room, the pillow around his ears, were now insignificant. His father had been cruelly beaten. Not outside. But on the inside he was black and blue and hurting. Jeff could see hurt in the hunched shoulders and the fingers gripping the whisky glass.

There was a movement in Jeff's chest, something like a bit of swallowed warmth, that flowed out into his arms. He didn't have to think about it. He opened the door, went out, and put his arm around his father's shoulders.

For a while Winston didn't move, then he put his glass down on the concrete and placed his hand over Jeff's. "You're a good kid." He patted Jeff's hand, then said in a flat voice. "It wasn't all my loss. I invested clients' money. I shouldn't have, but I was going to repay it with interest before the end of the year. If I don't get it back, well, the truth is, Jeffrey, we'll have to sell this house."

8

IN MATHEMATICS, THE FIBONACCI NUMBERS, or Fibonacci series, are the numbers in the following integer sequence: 0, 1, 1, 2, 3, 5, 8, 13, 21, 34, 55, 89, 144 ... The first number is 0. The second number is 1. Each subsequent number is the sum of the previous two. The Fibonacci pattern of numbers is often found in nature, in leaf arrangement, tree branches, flower petals, sunflower seed heads and pine cones.

Jeff had discovered that there were currents of events that escaped logical planning. For example, if you couldn't think of a word you let it go and soon after, some tide would wash it up, unbidden, on the shores of your mind. It was the same with wanting something. You could chase it, like a dog after a cat, and all you did was wear yourself out. Give up the chase, and it came to you. There were no rules about this. No one, to the best of his knowledge, had come up with a formula of possibilities for this phenomenon. It just happened.

After a week of desperately seeking Maisie, he gave up. Some of the crazy things she'd said were making sense in a weird sort of way. Andy had left school. Winston in quicksand? Well, maybe debt could suck you under. But what did she mean about Helen on a cliff edge? Was that about an accident or something else? Jeff was full of questions. There were things he'd half forgotten. He needed her to repeat them. He also needed her full name again, and address so he could visit her. Searching the city was a waste of time. He went to the library every day after school. He even stood against the verandah post outside the Chinese restaurant, but she didn't appear. He didn't know what else to do.

He met Andrea at McDonald's and although she was smiling and lively, he was aware of a jittery distance between them.

"Beck is coming tomorrow," she said.

"I know."

"He's flying in with a police escort and he's going to that new prison. Mark is going to help me get to Auckland to see him."

He wanted to say, what about me, but he didn't.

Andy unwrapped her burger. "Did you see his photo in the paper? He's lost a lot of weight. His hair is short. He looks a lot older."

Jeff wasn't hungry. He nudged the chicken wrap in front of him. "She told me you would leave school. That old woman. She told me, and you said —"

"Jeff, don't have anything to do with that crazy creature! She's demonic!"

He continued, "I asked you if you were going to leave and you laughed at me. You said of course not."

Her eyes softened. "Oh, Squidgy, I had to go. I felt rotten leaving you, but look, one day you can come and live with us, Mark and me. Mark is amazingly kind and considerate. He's always thinking about other people, and you know what? He loves me exactly as I am, and Jeff, I am so in love with him!"

He picked up a chip and then dropped it back in the packet. "What about the law degree?"

She wiped her mouth with a paper napkin. "I've left school. There's no turning back. If I was going to change my mind, Mum made sure I didn't. She went to the school and cleared my desk and locker. Did you know that?"

He nodded. "Yeah. She found the letters from Beck."

"Oh! Trust her to snoop! Well, that's no longer important, thank goodness. No more hiding things. I'm in the process of getting a job."

"Where?"

"I've got two interviews coming up, the restaurant at the Klaxton Hotel and the museum café. Aren't you going to eat that?"

He looked at her. "Dad has to sell the house."

"What?"

"If he doesn't get the money back, he's in trouble. Big trouble. He invested money belonging to some of his clients." Jeff broke a chip in half. "Even if he does sell the house, it's got a mortgage. There mightn't be enough left over to buy something else."

She leaned towards him. "What does Mum think of that?"

"Not much."

"I know. More arguments, more cat and dog fights."

His throat was closing up and he was close to tears, but he had to say it. "It might help if you came back."

"Not a hope!" she said. "I'm truly sorry, Squidgy, but that won't happen. Never!"

"At least talk to Mum."

"I'll do that when she stops calling me names." She reached across the table. "If you aren't hungry, I'll take that chicken wrap for my dinner tonight."

He pushed the food towards her hand. "Don't you eat with – you know, Mark?

She wrapped it in a paper serviette. "Not always," she said. "Sometimes he has dinner with his children."

"Children?"

She put the food in her bag. "He's been separated from his wife for over a year. She's a very cold woman. But he's a good father. It's nice to know there are some good fathers in the world. You take care, little brother." She got up, hoisted her bag straps over her shoulder, then bent over to kiss his cheek. "I'll text you about Beck."

He stayed seated after she had gone and didn't move until an attendant came to wipe down the table. By then, he'd been sitting so long that one leg had gone to sleep. His sister might be in love but there wasn't much of it leaking out. He limped down to the bus stop and caught the next bus to the bottom of the hill. He felt tired. He felt empty, as though something had drained all his blood.

He got off the bus, his pulse pumping air in his ears, and there, in the glass shelter waiting for him, was Maisie.

* * *

He'd got used to her smile, the broken grey teeth edged with black and the way her eyes narrowed to shards of dark glass.

"Maisie, I'm so glad —" He stopped. He didn't know what he was glad about, only that seeing her made a difference. But he had to admit he was still not one hundred per cent sure of the dream-keeper story. Was she an old lady like Great-aunt Rose, imagining things? He dared to ask the question. "Are you really Maisie?"

"At the risk of repeating myself, Maisie left the

dream weeks ago. I thought I'd made that clear. She gave me permission to use the body she was leaving." The woman hit her stick against the concrete. "But use is not the word for something useless."

"So what do you want me to call you? Maisie? Dream-keeper?"

She put out her hand and touched his face. Her fingers were cold against his cheek. "I told you, Maisie will do. Dream-keepers don't have individual names. They're a category."

He scratched the back of his neck. "Do you like being Maisie?"

"Like? What is there to like? Arthritis, deafness, memory loss, palpitations and now, kidney failure!" She drummed her stick at each ailment. "It's like jumping into a car that's ready for the scrap heap."

"I mean, do you like being human?" He was looking directly into her eyes. When she didn't answer, didn't blink, he said, "You don't look sick. You have a lot of energy."

"That's the fuel that goes into the car," she said. "But it's the state of the car that counts." She leaned towards him. "This is rent-a-wreck. The engine's had it. Do I have to spell it out? I can't be in your dream much longer, Number Nine."

For a couple of seconds he studied the thin, lined face and the intense eyes. There was so much he wanted to know. "You said things. They didn't make sense, before. But now – now I've got feelings about them and I've got questions."

"What do you want to ask?"

He hesitated, then said, "How did you know about my family?"

"There's no copyright on knowledge," she snapped. Then she turned her head to look at the sea. "It's my job, Jeff, and there are ways of knowing that are beyond the function of a small human brain. For example, I understand the bond between you and your brother. When you think about him there is pain in your upper chest and arms. Right?"

He nodded, suddenly afraid. No one but he could possibly know how he felt when people talked about Beckett.

"But your clever little brain hasn't worked out why the pain should happen. Has it?

This time, he shook his head.

"So that's my answer," she said. "You can't understand how I know about your family, but at least you can accept the limitations of the human brain. Now what's the next question?"

He opened his school backpack. "Is it okay if I write things down?"

"As long as you're fast about it," she said.

He took the notepad out so quickly that his bag dropped to the floor of the bus shelter and books slid out. He didn't pick them up.

"Where do you live?"

"Number 7B Aurora Council Flats, Newtown."

"Nine!" he said. "That's perfect!"

"What?"

"B is two. Add two to seven and you have –"

"All right, all right. What else?"

He held the pen ready. "What exactly, is the definition of a dream-keeper?"

"I've told you many times."

"I know. But now I want to write it down."

"It's a spirit that comes into the dream. It inhabits a body – a person, or maybe an animal."

He wrote a few sentences then said, "That sounds more like a movie than something real."

Her smile came back. "Real! Remember what I said about limited understanding? You think this little life is reality? Fiddlesticks!" She clenched the stick between her knees and threw up her hands. "How many times do I have to tell you! It's about ten per cent of reality. The moment you get a body you lose the memory of the other ninety per cent. Even if you don't understand that, you'd better believe it." She turned on the seat so that she was facing him. "In the dream you call life you know only what comes through your five senses. Right?"

He nodded. "What I see, hear, taste, touch, smell."

"So in the dream you think you know everything. You don't. You know only what your body allows you to know. The other ninety per cent is the realm of spirit."

For a moment he was acutely aware of colour and form, the folds in her padded jacket, the green-and-orange dress that lay around her thin legs, the small bushes outside that collected bits of paper and other rubbish, and the smell of the sea that rolled against land and sky. In that moment, it seemed that his senses were bombarded with information. He looked down at his notes and said to her, "My sister Andrea thinks you're some kind of devil."

He wondered if she'd be offended, but she thought it funny. She laughed and slapped her knee. "Your sister shouldn't believe everything she thinks! Devil or angel depends on the kind of human judgements you make. It has nothing to do with the reality."

"But you and me sitting here. Isn't this reality?"

"No, no!" She looked frustrated. "It's only a small part of it! Jeff, you are a spirit renting a body for a short time in order to add to the increase of Light. You come with a plan – the body you will inhabit, the tools you will have, and the growth you need to accomplish. Some spirits have a modest plan. They take on a body for a short time, or they choose a path that is not too demanding. Others are more ambitious." She was talking so fast, she was spitting through the gaps in her teeth. "A difficult path has greater growth potential, but it can be dangerous. You see, Number Nine, when you take on a body there's the forgetting. Suddenly, the spirit is a prisoner to body experience and it doesn't remember —"

"Stop!" he said. "You went too fast." He lifted the pen. "I can't write all that!"

"Then write this down," she said. "Your family chose demanding paths and now they're in grave danger because they have lost the memory."

"Memory?" He paused at the word.

"The other way of knowing. I said that when you come into a body, there is a forgetting. That's true. But every spirit brings a spark of the Light with it. The Light is a guide, like a compass. It's a little memory of the big reality. In the dream, people call it heart knowledge, although it has nothing to do with the muscle that pumps blood."

He said slowly, deliberately, "What exactly — does — a — dream-keeper — do?"

"Oh! Shut your cakehole, Number Nine!" she snapped. "You keep saying you don't understand, and when I try to explain, you interrupt —"

"I need to know."

Now she was annoyed with him. "A dream-keeper is a nanny, guardian, shepherd, tour guide, angel, advisor. We are spirits. When the dreams are in danger of becoming nightmares, we jump in. But we can only work with someone who hasn't lost the memory. That's you, Jeff. You still know the Light within you. So it's my job to help you. Your task is to fan your Light into a flame. Got that? It will bring back the memory of Light to your entire family."

He thought for a while. "You mean love? That's it, isn't it? Love!"

"You found a good word for it. There are others: forgiveness, compassion, empathy! But the words are just words unless they connect with the Light in you. Write that down, too."

He wrote hastily, hoping he would be able to read it. This is like a story, he thought as he wrote, like some kind of myth or legend. Parts of it felt right.

She coughed and wiped her mouth on her sleeve. "The reality is too big for human language. At school you learn about metaphor, allegory, parable. Well, don't you? Okay. The words themselves don't really matter. When they match the Light in you, you will respond to them. You'll get what you call a feeling. Is there anything else you want to know?"

He knew there was a multitude of new questions that would attack him as soon as he got home, but right now, he couldn't think of one. He said, "You told me things that have happened, like Dad in the quicksand. I suppose that was a metaphor, but Andrea's was real. She left school. Everything has changed. Mum goes between crying and shouting. Beckett is coming back to New Zealand and our house has to be sold. Is anything else going to happen?"

She looked at him, her eyes bright and unblinking. "Yes," she said. "There is more to come. It's up to you, Jeff. When it's time, you'll do what you need to do. But it will be without me. I can't stay in the dream much longer."

"You mean you are going to die."

At that, she began to laugh, a rumble in her chest that reached her mouth and eyes and then shook her entire body. She coughed and whacked her stick against the concrete. "There is no such thing as death," she said.

* * *

Mrs Wilson could be tough. She gave Jeff five out of ten for his project on Dmitri Mendeleev, saying that the topic given was a historical figure, not the significance of the periodic table. He was disappointed and indignant, disappointed for himself, and indignant that Mendeleev's achievement should be dismissed like that. But then Mrs Wilson was not a physicist. Paul got nine out of ten for writing about Henry VIII, who achieved practically nothing worthwhile, and Salosa got a full ten for six pages on Captain Cook. Jeff was pleased for them both. His five out of ten was an explosion of red ink, not done with Mrs Wilson's birthday pen, nor by a good Russian pencil. He supposed it really didn't matter. If he had to rate his personal disappointment on the same scale, it would be two out of ten, small compared with other events in his life that hit the full score.

At lunch break, it was raining, and he sat in the recreation room with his sandwiches and his notebook, trying to ignore the noise around him. This was the day Beck was flying in, and no one in the family would be at the airport to see him. I'm sorry, Beck, he whispered to himself. I'm so horribly, terribly, awfully sorry.

He looked at his notes. He hadn't written all the old woman had said, but the words he'd scribbled prompted his memory and he was able to fill most of the blanks. It wasn't craziness, he decided. It was a story, like Maui and his brothers netting the sun, like Orpheus going into the underworld to find that girl with the strange name. It was one of those stories that had echoes in it, vibrations, like patterns of numbers. The patterns meant something but he didn't know what. Maybe only a "dream-keeper" could offer a mathematical sequence that made sense of the story.

He read the notes again and underlined two things that seemed engraved inside him. *It's up to you, Jeff. Light.* The words escaped his brain but they were in his chest and stomach, and he didn't know what to do with them.

Someone was standing in front of him. "Hey! Jeffrey Lorimer!"

He raised his head and saw it was Clive.

"Your brother is Beckett Lorimer, right? The drug dealer?"

"Yes."

"My father says taxpayers' dollars are rescuing him from a prison in Thailand."

"Yes. I suppose so." He saw a gleam in the stare, heard the voice reaching for every ear in the recreation room.

"More taxpayers' dollars for keeping him in that flash new prison in Auckland," Clive announced.

Jeff shrugged. "A prison is still a prison." He looked down at his notes.

But Clive hadn't finished. "Your sister, Andrea. She's living with a married man. He's got two kids. My parents know his wife. What's wrong with your family?"

Everyone was watching, waiting for his answer. Jeff felt very tired. The only thing he could think of was something the old woman had thrown at him yesterday. "Shut your cakehole," he said.

⋆ ⋆ ⋆

He went to Paul's place after school, to have another session on the drums, do homework, anything to avoid going straight home. Mr Fitzgibbon and the dog were in the backyard. He was mulching the vegetable garden, and the dog, scratching in the compost, had rotting plants over its nose and muzzle. Mr Fitzgibbon stopped to ask Jeff how things were. Jeff wasn't sure what he meant, but guessed he'd heard something, so he told him about Mr Staunton-Jones. Mr Fitzgibbon didn't know, and he looked shocked. "One and a half million dollars!" he exclaimed as though that was all the money in the world. "What a terrible thing to happen!"

Jeff nodded. Mr Fitzgibbon was very tall, and up close, Jeff was talking to faded blue jeans and gumboots crusted with compost. "It's really awful," he said, patting the dog. "We thought he was such a kind man. He fooled everyone."

Mr Fitzgibbon put his hand on Jeff's shoulder. "Nearly always, evil tries to disguise itself as virtue. Tell your dad we'll pray for him, if he thinks that will help."

You don't know my father, Jeff wanted to say, he's allergic to stuff like that, but instead he nodded again. He didn't want to upset Mr Fitzgibbon further by telling him that the police weren't doing anything fast, and Dad had to sell their house to pay back his clients. That would have been too much. He turned and went inside to see Paul.

★ ★ ★

Helen's first words were, "Where have you been?"

"Paul's," he said. "Mr Fitzgibbon drove me home."

"Why didn't you send me a text? You know the rules."

"I forgot." That was true. Getting in touch had been the last thing on his mind.

She slammed a cupboard door. "Do you know what's happened? Your idiot father has invited a land agent to look at the house. What do you think of that?"

He didn't answer.

She said in a louder voice. "I said your idiot of a father is selling our home. This place is half mine, but was I consulted? Of course not!"

Jeff knew she wasn't talking to him, but to Winston who was somewhere near, probably in his office. He was right. His father came into the living room, walking unevenly. His eyes were red. He had been drinking. "You're a bit late, son," he said to Jeff.

"It's a pretty picture, isn't it?" Helen said. "The financial genius who was going to buy — what was it? A villa in Tuscany? An island in Fiji?"

Winston swayed slightly and put his hand on the back of a chair to steady himself. "Don't!" he bellowed. "Do not make me the criminal! This was an — an investment in good faith. I did everything I could —"

"Good faith!" She spat the words back at him. "You played up to him. You saw him as an old rich man who was giving you his property cheap, because you were like a son. Yes, Daddy Warren. I'll look after your beautiful little kingdom, Daddy Warren. But as soon as it was yours, you planned to sell it to the developers."

"It was an investment!" Winston looked confused. He put his hand up in a helpless gesture as though he was trying to clear the air of words. "I did it for you, Helen! I did it for my family!"

"No! You did it for greed," said Helen, "and now your family will be homeless."

He lurched forward, angry now. "Will you bloody well shut up? We'll get the money back. Eventually. Until then we can rent a house." He held his hands out to her, his voice shaking. "All of it, Helen, everything I did, was for family!"

"You have no family, Winston," she said.

"Stop!" Jeff cried. "Stop it!"

"You destroyed us!" Helen said. "Your children, one by one, and now me. Yes, me, Winston Lorimer! If this house goes, so do I."

Winston hit her.

His fist came up twice. She shrieked, spun around and with the second blow, fell to the floor.

Jeff ran to his mother. She was on her back. Her arms and legs were at sharp angles against the white marble tiles. Her lip was bleeding down the side of her face, but she wasn't knocked out. Jeff took her left arm and helped her into a sitting position. She was crying. There was a red mark on her left cheek.

He turned to his father, who was still standing by the chair. "Dad!"

Winston stepped backwards, shaking his head, little shakes as though he didn't believe any of it.

Helen stood up, touched her mouth and looked at the red on her fingers. "That does it," she said, and went to the bathroom.

Jeff was now crying, huge gulping sobs. "Why, Dad? Why did you hit her?"

Winston sat heavily in the chair, staring at him, but it seemed to Jeff that he wasn't seeing anything. "What a bloody mess," he growled.

After a long time, Helen came out of the north wing of the house, wheeling an overnight bag. Her lip was still oozing blood. She ignored Winston, and said to Jeff, "I've booked a motel. Grab a few things, Jeffrey, just enough for the night. We'll collect the rest tomorrow."

Winston looked at her, but said nothing.

"Please, Mum," Jeff said. "Please, don't!"

"I said, pack a bag. Come on, Jeffrey. Hurry up! We're getting out of this hellhole."

"I don't want to go," Fresh tears were spilling. "Mum, let's stay. Please?"

"We are going!" She nudged her bag against his leg. "Do as I tell you!"

He felt that all his insides were being torn up like bits of paper and tossed into the wind. But there was something else in him, something strong that remained. He walked over to Winston who was sitting as still as a rock, and put his hand on his shoulder. "No, Mum," he said, "I'm staying with Dad."

9

IN 1632, GALILEO GAVE AN EXPLANATION OF TIDES in a work he called "Dialogue on the Tides". His theory was incorrect because he attributed tides to sloshing water caused by Earth's movements around the sun. At the same time, Johannes Kepler correctly suggested that the moon caused tides. Isaac Newton was the first person to explain tides as the product of the gravitational pull of astronomical masses.

At seven-thirty in the morning, Winston was still in his pyjamas. His face was grey and stubbled and he looked hung-over.

Jeff helped himself to muesli then cut a banana over it. "Aren't you going to work?"

"Not this morning. There's a land agent coming. Don't forget to wash your dishes. Do you know where your mother keeps the coffee?"

"I think we're out. There's no bread, either. I'll have

to buy my lunch." He looked up. "Dad, I'll need to buy something for lunch."

His father walked out of the room and after a while came back with a fistful of coins and notes. He dropped them on the table.

"That's too much!" Jeff said.

"So? Treat yourself. Buy chocolate or something."

"Dad!" Jeff spread the money across the table. "There's over sixty dollars here. I don't want it. Twenty is more than enough."

"Take it while you can. Before it all runs out. Before we're begging in the streets." His father shoved the morning paper in front of him. "See this?"

It was folded at the third page and there, at the top, was a photo of a man between two police officers. The man was Beckett and the background was Auckland Airport.

Jeff counted the raisins in his muesli. Usually there were between seven and ten, but today was bottom of the packet, and raisins sank, being heavy, so there would be at least twenty.

"I don't deserve this," Winston said, his forefinger stabbing the photo. "I don't deserve any of it. What happened to right and wrong? My dad had good old-fashioned values. If I stepped out of line, it was his belt. I respected that. Once, he caught me smoking in the woodshed. I tell you, I couldn't sit down for a week. Mark my words, it didn't do me any harm. So what's changed? Huh? Where's the respect?"

Fourteen, fifteen. The muesli was thick with raisins. There could be more than twenty.

"I never hit her before," Winston said. "I despise men who hit women. But, you know, she's got a tongue like a razor. She went on and on. Don't tell me. I know it's no excuse. The thing is, she and I need to talk now. Communication, that's what. Did she phone this morning?"

Jeff nodded.

His head tipped quickly, like a bird's. "What did she say?"

"She wanted to know if I was all right." Eighteen, nineteen, twenty.

"Is she coming back today?"

Raisins were dried grapes. They lost their juice and wrinkled but they didn't give up their sweetness. They were like sugar between the teeth. "I don't know," he said.

"Did she tell you the name of the motel?"

"No."

"Well, that's bloody lovely," Winston rocked back in his chair. "How do I talk to her then? You know I didn't mean to hit her. You do know that, son. And you do believe that everything I've done has been for this family?"

Jeff hoped there would be twenty-seven raisins, but the final number, twenty-one, was just as good.

That came to three, Beck's number.

His father picked up a spoon and turned it between his fingers. "I have to put the house on the market. It can take weeks, months to sell. I can't risk delay. She must know that. We'll rent an ordinary family home and when the police get off their backsides, we'll get our money back. What your mother doesn't understand is the setback is only temporary. We'll buy or build something just as nice as this."

Jeff glanced again at the photo in the paper. It was Beck, all right, but different, older, thinner, with short hair and lines at the edge of his mouth.

What had happened to the long blond hair that swished about when he laughed?

"Talk to her, will you?" Winston was saying. "Tell her I need to see her. Can you do that for me?"

He nodded. "Okay."

Winston put his elbows on the table, his head in his hands. "The silly woman has been talking about divorce."

* * *

His phone was buzzing with messages from his mother and Andrea, wanting to know if he was all right. He didn't know if he was all right. He remembered a scene from a movie, a man in a space suit who had been working on the outside of the spacecraft when he got cut loose. He had whirled away, head over heels like some big snowman, disappearing into blackness. That was how Jeff felt, but there were no exact words for it. Lost in space was metaphor or allegory, he wasn't sure which.

Phones were not allowed in school, but they could be switched off and stored in lockers. He closed down messages without reading them and went early into the classroom to avoid the stares of students in the school grounds. It seemed that even the little kids knew about his brother.

Mrs Wilson was sitting at her desk. "Good morning, Jeffrey."

"Good morning, Mrs Wilson."

"Cool morning, isn't it? Autumnal! Out goes cricket and in comes rugby." Her mouth smiled at him. Her eyes looked anxious. "How are you, Jeffrey. I mean, really, how are you?"

"All right," he smiled back. "Thank you, Mrs Wilson."

"Is there anything you want to tell me?"

He shook his head.

"I don't know about you, but when I've got something on my mind, it helps to have a chat about it." She folded her arms and leaned back in her chair. "Not someone close. The people close to me will already have opinions. No, I go to a person who isn't involved. I talk to someone I trust. Maybe they'll see the problem more clearly from a distance. I find that very useful."

He nodded in agreement but didn't say anything.

"Jeffrey, we all have challenges, and we sometimes need help to deal with them. I wonder if you, well, I mean would you like an appointment with the school counsellor?"

This time, he shook his head.

"Are you sure? She is good at her job. You can absolutely trust her."

He shook his head again.

Mrs Wilson looked ready to cry. "I've talked to some of my colleagues and we're very concerned about our lovely Jeffrey. We know things aren't easy for you, dear, and we —"

"I've got a counsellor," he said.

"You have?"

"Yes. Someone I can talk to."

"I'm very pleased to hear it. Did your parents arrange that for you? I'm sure you'll find it very worthwhile. Who is your counsellor?"

He heard the thunder of feet in the hallway and he glanced at the door. "Her name is Maisie," he said.

★   ★   ★

After school he went to Argonaut Travel, and yes, his mother was at her desk, working on the computer.

She wore make-up that covered the bruise on her cheek, but lipstick didn't hide the brown ridge and swelling on her upper lip. She spoke in a low voice, "Jeffrey, I don't want you to spend another night with him. He's unpredictable. He's dangerous. I'm looking for a house. Three bedrooms. I think Andrea might stay with us and go back to school."

"Dad didn't mean it," he said.

"He has always been a bully," she said. "I'm thankful I held on to this job. I've got a small amount put away, enough for a bond and a month's rent in advance. We'll manage, and it will be better, Jeffrey, I promise you."

He shifted from one foot to another. "When do you finish? Can you drive me home?"

She saw through that and gave him a long look. "No, Jeffrey. I went up to the house today and got most of my clothes."

"Did you talk to Dad?"

"No. He talked to me – the way he usually talks. At me. Further communication can be through lawyers." She leaned towards him.

"I want you to come back to the motel with me."

He was stuck, unable to say yes or no.

"Are you listening, Jeffrey?"

He didn't want to hurt her. He didn't want to make her angry. "Please," he said. "Come home, Mum. Just for tonight."

"It won't change anything." She shook her head. "It's over, Jeffrey. Do you realise that I legally own half that house? That man refuses to even consider my legal rights. All he thinks about is himself, and that's the way it's always been." Tears came into her eyes.

Jeff was aware that the women at the next desk were listening. They probably knew everything, anyway. "Please, Mum," he whispered.

"Tonight you stay with me," Helen said.

At that moment, he saw something clearly that he had not seen before. They were the same, Winston, Helen, Andrea, they all thought only about themselves. They were like little islands. That's why we aren't a family, he thought. No one really cares about anyone else. He wasn't sure about Beck. Maybe Beckett cared. It was hard to tell, not having seen him for a long time.

"I can't, Mum," he said. "I really need to stay with Dad." Then he left before the other women could see he was crying.

* * *

He hoped that Maisie would be at the bus stop again, but didn't really expect it. She had warned him that he might not see her again. He walked up the hill and long before he reached the gates of his house, he saw the red-and-white FOR SALE signs. Too fast, he thought. It is all happening too fast.

Winston was waiting for him at the door. He was dressed in shorts and a floral shirt, and his breath smelled of drink.

Jeff hated the whisky smell that seemed to him to be a mixture of petrol and perfume. "Did you go to work?" he asked.

"I did, indeed." Winston swayed. "But I came home for my son. Yeah. I did. Couldn't have you, you know ..." He paused, groped for words, "... come home to an empty house."

Jeff thought, but I usually come home to an empty house, and then he decided it was wrong to even think it. His father was trying to be friendly. He said, "I saw the sign."

"We're looking up," said Winston. "Son, I think we've turned the corner. Two bits of news! The land agent thinks this house will go in days. Unique, he said. One of a kind! He's got Asian buyers. Waiting for harbour views. While he was here, that lanky detective called. You know something? That lowlife Julius Clarke, he didn't go to England. No. He's been seen in Morocco. They're on to him." Winston paused, then said in a tired voice, "You're a good son, Jeffrey."

Jeff looked around the room. It had been tidied.

Winston went on, "You'll be sad about the house

being sold. But mark my words, there'll be another. Just as good."

"I liked the old place we had before," Jeff said. "It was cosy, like a real home."

"That's the kind of house we'll be renting. Four bed, two bath, neighbours over the back fence! Not for long, though." He poured himself another drink. "Let's go out and celebrate. Dinner at Dockside!"

"I can cook something," Jeff offered.

"No, no! If a man can't take his son out for a meal, there's something wrong. Get changed. Comb your hair. While you're at it, give your mother a call. Invite her too."

Jeff said, "I don't think she'll come."

"She might. She might not. We don't know unless we ask." Winston smiled. "She'll get over it. It's happened before. Emotional! Women don't think the way men do. Tell her we've got good news to celebrate."

"Dad, I'm sure she won't come."

"Shall we see who's right?" Winston winked at him.

Jeff was right, and by the time Helen had answered the message with *R U joking*, Winston was asleep in one of the recliner chairs.

About nine o'clock, Jeff opened a can of spaghetti and had it on toast.

* * *

The land agent's prediction was correct, and before the week was out, a couple bought the big house with its view across the harbour. The settlement date was the fifteenth of May, which would allow Winston four weeks to find a rental house in town and call in a removal company. There was enough furniture to fill a normal house plus two garages, so some of it would have to be put in storage.

As for everything else, it seemed to Jeff that the changes had ceased. It was like that game of statues, where everyone dances about while the music plays, and freezes when it stops. Events that had happened in rapid succession, one change after another, had become stuck in one place.

He counted the stuck-ness on his fingers. One, the police had no further news. Two, Helen was still in a motel and wouldn't communicate with Winston except through a lawyer. Three, Andrea's life was full of a man called Mark and she had not yet been to see Beckett, although he'd been in Auckland nearly two weeks. Four, Winston went to work each day and came home early so no one could say that Jeff was left on his own. Five, school was the same, kids staring, whispering.

Jeff got used to it, the ebb and flow of each day, currents moving in set patterns.

Although Winston opened the newspaper at rental properties, he didn't do anything about finding a house. He was more concerned about Helen and her lawyer. Helen stayed on at the motel because, she said, she got a discount through the travel agency and there were no suitable properties at the moment.

The only thing to happen in that week was Andrea's interviews. She missed both waitressing jobs but found work packing shelves in a supermarket. When Jeff met her in the car park, she was wearing a pink uniform. "It'll do until something else comes along," she said. "There's not much work around."

He wondered if there could be a vacancy for her in Argonaut Travel.

"Ask my mother for a job? I'd rather scrub toilets! No, I'm fine. I'm earning money and that's important because I can't be a burden to Mark. His ex is a dentist and she makes a mint. But he still has to pay maintenance for the children." Anger burned in her eyes. "She's an awful woman. I don't know why he married her."

Jeff felt uncomfortable with this new Andrea. He asked, "Have you heard from Beck?"

"Who? Oh, Beck! Yes, he wrote last week. He addresses all my letters care of Marlena, but she's still at school. I didn't get it for several days. He's fine. It's that new prison. He's glad to be back in New Zealand."

For Jeff, this wasn't enough. Had she forgotten her promises? But he tried to sound reasonable. "Did Beck say anything about us going to Auckland go see him?"

"That's impossible right now. No money." She examined her purple painted nails. "Really, he's fine. Look Jeff, I'd better go. Mark will be home soon."

"Wasn't there any news?" Jeff pleaded. "Did he write about the flight back? What happened at the airport? You know? TV cameras and reporters? He must have said something."

"It was all okay. He said he might be helping out in the kitchen."

"What kitchen? The prison? Andy, I want to see his letter."

"I haven't got it."

"What?"

"I mean I haven't got it now." She waved her hands at him. "Don't bug me, Jeff!"

"Then, please, please, tell me the address! I've got to write to him. Seriously, Andy! I know I have to –"

But she was in too much of a hurry. "I've forgotten, but I'll write it down for the next time I see you. Promise. Bye, Squidge."

* * *

Saturday morning was the beginning of the school holidays. He knew what he had to do. As usual, he counted the steps down the hill to the bus stop, and waited; but this time he took the bus that went through Newtown. Maisie had given the address as

Aurora Council Flats, but in the white pages, it was listed as Aurora Retirement Village, and since the street was the same, that had to be it. He got off the bus in the Newtown shopping centre and walked to the road. It was short and had no exit. From the corner, he could see the word *AURORA* over an open gateway. It was impossible to miss.

Inside there were two rows of green painted units wedged together with carports, a small garden in front of each. Along the drive were a few big trees standing in their fallen leaves. Everything was wet. He walked along the B row, stopped outside the door that had a large 7 on it and knocked. There was no answer. He knocked again and again.

The door of Number 6 opened and a man crouched over a walking frame said, "No one's home. That's empty."

"I'm looking for Mrs Eleanor May Caldwell. I think this is supposed to be her flat."

"It's Miss," the man said, "and she's been moved to the hospital wing."

Jeff's breath caught on the word hospital. So she was sick. How sick? He stepped back. "Thank you. Can you tell me where it is?"

"Down the end. You'll see it." The man waved his hand and then backed into the unit, dragging the walking frame after him.

Jeff walked along the drive in front of the other

B units, twenty-eight in all. The concrete was cracked and uneven, with holes filled with gravel. He needed to watch where he trod. The air held drops of moisture that were more than mist and less than rain, and his ears were cold.

The hospital was also an old green-painted building, but designed like a large house with a turnaround drive and wheelchair access. When he opened the door, there was a blast of warm air, and he walked into a reception area with a floral carpet and three chairs opposite an alcove where a large woman sat behind a counter. "Hello, dear," she said. "Are you looking for someone?"

Her friendliness warmed him. "Yes. Miss Eleanor May Caldwell."

"Who?" She looked puzzled for a second and then her face cleared.

"Oh, you mean Maisie!"

"Yes!"

The woman consulted her computer. Her smile faded and she folded her hands. "Are you related, dear? Family?"

He nodded.

"Is anyone with you?"

"No." He hesitated. "Mum's working."

"You know she is poorly, don't you, dear. Twenty-four-hour care. You can see her if you want to, but she won't recognise you. She's in a coma."

He wiped his hands on his jeans. "I'd like to see her. She — she's special."

"Come with me, dear, and I'll take you down. It's lovely of you to come. Are you her grandson? No, you'll be a great-grandson. When was the last time you saw our Maisie?"

He counted. "Nearly two weeks ago."

"Then you'll know what to expect. What's your name, dear?"

"Jeff."

"Down this way, Jeff. Maisie is quite a character. We thought we were losing her a few weeks ago, but she made a remarkable recovery." She paused, her hand on a doorknob. "This time, though, she is slipping away." The door opened inwards. "Come in, Jeff."

It was a small room, hot and stuffy and smelling bad. Maisie lay on her back on a narrow white bed, only her head visible. Without the usual hat, it was the small head he'd seen under the gum tree. There were wisps of grey hair and a thin face that reminded him of a bird. Her mouth hung open in a down-turned crescent, and her eyes, half open, had rolled back so he saw only the whites, which weren't white but a greyish yellow. He could hear her breathing.

Beside the bed, a nurse sat in a chair, knitting red wool. She looked up and the kindly woman who'd brought him in said, "This is Jeff. He's here to see his great-grandmother."

The nurse smiled, gathered her knitting, and stood, indicating the chair for Jeff. "Doesn't she look nice?" she said, nodding at the bed. "So peaceful."

For a moment Jeff and the two women stood looking at Maisie. Sunlight penetrating grey mist caused a patch of pale light to fall through the glass, marking a window shape on the bedcover. Under it, Maisie's body made a mound so small that she looked already half gone. Jeff knew it wasn't Maisie. Eleanor May Caldwell had left this body more than a month ago, and now the dream-keeper was struggling to free itself. He knew all that, but he still felt sad. In his mind, Maisie and the dream-keeper were like the same person.

The nurse said, "You can talk to her if you like. She might still be able to hear you."

"She doesn't have long to go," the receptionist said. "Hours, days. Not long at all. Jeff, we'll pop out for a few minutes. If you need us, press this buzzer."

They went out quietly, and he sat in the chair next to her, counting the uneven breaths. She did look peaceful, but she was in some place far away and she wouldn't come back. Tears burned in his throat. Everyone was now at a distance, Helen, Winston, Andrea, Beck, the kids at school. Or maybe he was the one who was far away, like that astronaut in the white suit, tumbling head over heels into the blackness of forever.

He said aloud, "I still don't understand that dream-keeper story. I think I do, but I don't. I came with more questions, Maisie, but it's too late. I'm really pleased for you, because I know you want to go. I know you're not Maisie but I need to call you something because you're my friend and you have to have a name."

Beyond the words, his mind was still counting the rise and fall of air from her mouth, two distinct sounds that sometimes got caught in her throat, one hundred and twenty-seven, one hundred and twenty-eight.

"Maisie, I think you can hear me." He leaned closer and there was that familiar pressure in his ears. "You know why I think that? I can feel the Light in you. Well, I suppose it's Light. I'm not sure what to call it. Something in you like – like energy. Only not as strong as before."

He was reminded of the Fitzgibbon basement, and Paul playing a song called "The River of Life". The title hadn't meant anything to Jeff, but now it came to him as images of water, little streams becoming rivers and rivers flowing towards the sea. Near the end of its journey, a river had a lot of salt water in it. How did people know where the river ended and the sea began?

He wanted to hold Maisie's hand, but her arms and hands were under the covers. There was only her head, barely denting the pillow. So he stood up, leaned over and kissed her on the forehead.

An amazing thing happened. Her eyes opened wide, dark and focused. She smiled, her mouth curving up. She was conscious, looking directly at him. She knew him! Those eyes black as coal, shone with silent laughter. It was a miracle!

"Maisie!" he said.

She didn't speak. The smile slowly faded, her eyes rolled up, the eyelids came down, and it was over. The breathing continued, steady but loud, air-in high-pitched, air-out deep and rough.

Outside, the mist was clearing and the sunlight fell across the bed, shining on the pillow, her face, her hair. He realised that he had stopped counting her breaths. It didn't matter. He didn't need to hold her by counting. Something better had happened.

He remembered two things underlined in his notebook. They were important, she had told him. Now he said those words aloud. "It's up to you, Jeff. Hold on to the Light." He turned from the bed and walked to the door.

There was no one in the corridor. He glanced back at her and saw the slight movement of the covers as her breath continued. He would leave the door ajar so that a nurse would see he had gone.

The reception desk was also empty. Maybe they were having a lunch break. Lunch was his next plan.

He would get a bus to the train station and walk across to the wharf to where Helen would be waiting with a plastic box of sandwiches. They would throw bits to the seagulls and pigeons and watch boats move through the inner harbour. He walked past the line of retirement units, his shoes crunching gravel. Life is like a river, he thought, trying to remember the tune and the rest of the words.

He felt sad and he felt happy, the two things at once, and both were good. It was as though Maisie had stopped the astronaut's fall into endless space.

★ ★ ★

Lunch with his mother disturbed his peace, for she was still angry – with Winston for selling the house, and with Andrea for making a fool of herself. "She's not happy," Helen said. "I can tell. It's not working out, which doesn't at all surprise me, and she's too proud to admit it. What is wrong with my children? You were all such sweet babies."

He tried to avoid her anger by saying nothing. Anyway, his mouth was busy with the food, curried egg sandwiches, and the sun was warm on his legs. The mist had lifted and sorted itself into small cloud shapes, white against blue, and there was no wind. Boats moored by the wharf were twinned by their reflections in sea as smooth as oil.

"If she had any sense," said Helen, "she would use the school holiday period to catch up on the work she's missed, and she'd go back to college next term."

He ripped a crust in two and tossed it to a gull. Instantly there was a flock of birds at his feet, gulls, pigeons and two of the ducks that had been swimming by the *Dominion Post* ferry. There was a great screeching and flapping and he didn't see what happened to the crust.

"Don't encourage them," said Helen. "They are full of disease. You should talk to your sister, Jeffrey."

"I do," he said.

"You know full well what I'm saying. Point out that she's throwing her life away on this – this worthless infatuation. She's more likely to listen to you than to her mother."

"Andy's in love."

"Love? She doesn't know the meaning of the word. She's seventeen, for heaven's sake. That man should be put in front of a firing squad."

The birds hopped closer, eyes alert. He wanted to throw them the rest of the sandwich but didn't dare.

"What's happening to you over the holidays?" Helen asked.

"Nothing much. We've got football trials, but I might do hockey this winter."

"You father – what's he doing? What's happening to the house?"

"He's working from home for the next two weeks." He put the half-eaten egg sandwich back in the lunch box and closed the lid. "I don't know about the house. Why don't you ask him?"

She didn't answer, and when he looked at her, he saw her mouth was tight. He started counting the birds in front of him, but the numbers kept changing. Finally, he said, "Good lunch, Mum."

Slowly she turned, looked at him and smiled. Then she combed his hair with her fingers. "When did you last get a haircut?" she said, and her face looked normal again.

★ ★ ★

On Sunday afternoon he went with Paul Fitzgibbon to the new Batman movie. Afterwards, Paul invited him back to the house, but he made the excuse, "I'm making dinner for Dad." That was the truth, but it was about more than dinner. Winston drank whisky every night and sometimes he forgot things, like leaving a cigar burning on the wooden table instead of the ashtray, and turning on the microwave when there was nothing in it. Jeff needed to be there in the evenings, no two ways about it. Also, after the movie he didn't think he could cope with the usual Fitzgibbon noise and Paul's father feeling sorry for him because the house was sold.

The truth was, he wouldn't be sorry to leave the place. He liked the view of the harbour, but the house itself was lonely and had always been that way. Maybe because it was too big, like a shopping mall or business centre; lots of glass, marble floors, and spaces too open to be comfortable.

The loneliness had increased these past weeks. There was no one to talk to. Mr Sorensen was not like Eddie, who was always interested in people. The new gardener was a silent worker who preferred plants. As for Winston, he spent a lot of time in the office or outside, looking over the harbour with his own thoughts. All the fiery rage about the Sydney fraud, about Helen and Andrea and Beckett, seemed to have died down to cold ash. He looked burnt out.

That Sunday, Jeff kept thinking about Maisie. He wondered if she was still breathing, and how he could find out. Would it be possible to go to her funeral? Because he'd never been to a funeral, all he knew was what he had seen in films. Would he have to prove that he was related to Maisie? It bothered him that he had allowed the people at Aurora hospital to think he was her great-grandson.

He thought about the way Maisie had laughed when she said there was no such thing as death. At the time, he thought she meant she would go on breathing day after day and not stop. Of course that wasn't it. It was about someone getting out of an old car that wouldn't go any more. What did she call it? Rent-a-wreck.

It was raining again, traffic hissing on wet streets and umbrellas poking people at the bus stop. He didn't have a waterproof jacket and by the time he'd walked up the hill, he was soaked to the skin and his hair was dripping in his eyes. He felt cold. He fumbled in a wet pocket for the electronic gate opener. He stopped by the gum tree and said out loud, "Maisie, I still don't know how you got in here."

Then he saw Andrea's car. The little Toyota was parked in the middle of the yard, glistening with rain.

10

A FALLING OBJECT REACHES TERMINAL VELOCITY when the sum of the drag force and buoyancy equals the downward force of gravity acting on the object. Since the net force on the object is then zero, the object has zero acceleration. Drag depends on the projected area and that is why objects with a large area relative to mass, such as parachutes, have a lower terminal velocity than objects with a small area relative to mass, such as bullets.

Andrea had come home. She sat at the table, her hands around a cup, her eyes dull from weeping. Winston was standing beside her, angry, but not with his daughter. "If I get my hands on him, he'll wish he'd never been born."

Neither seemed to notice Jeff, who went to the fridge for a chocolate milk. Andrea put her head down in a fresh bout of crying and said, "It wasn't him, Dad. It was me."

Mark had gone back to his wife. Jeff knew something dramatic had happened when he saw the suitcases on the back seat of her car.

He wanted to feel sorry, but he couldn't. He wasn't the least bit sorry. He took his chocolate milk to the table and sat opposite her. "Hi, Andy."

She didn't look at him. Her long hair was loose around her face and she was wearing her blue T-shirt with the words *Don't tell me to have a nice day*, which would have been be funny if she weren't so unhappy. Winston stood near, hands in pockets, his mouth twitching as though it wanted to say something but he couldn't allow it.

"Are you hungry?" Jeff said. "There are pizzas in the freezer."

Andrea looked at him and her eyes filled up again. "He missed his children. That's the only reason."

He wanted to hug her but couldn't reach that far, so he grabbed her wrists. "We missed you, Andy. It's cool you're back. What do you want? Hawaiian, Pepperoni or Seafood? They're the thin-crust pizzas you like."

"Oh, shut up, Squidge," she said, and she put her head back down on her arms.

Winston turned to Jeff. "Call your mother, there's a good lad."

He wanted to tell his father that it wouldn't work. Helen was not returning. The marks on her face had faded, but they were still inside her like deep cuts with ugly scar tissue. Even her voice was different, hard and determined and there was no way you could argue past it.

But there was pleading in his father's eyes, so he made the call.

It was as he suspected. Helen was interested only in being proved right where Andrea was concerned. "This is not my problem," she said. "If she's old enough to create a mess in her life, she's old enough to clean it up."

* * *

The next morning, Andrea was reluctant to talk about the break-up. She was more or less back to normal, but she seemed older, quieter. At breakfast, she told Jeff there was no point in unpacking her suitcases.

He felt alarm. "You're not going again!"

"We're all going! Well, aren't we? Don't we have to move out of here in two weeks?"

He nodded.

"No one would think it. You and Dad have turned the place it into a pigsty. What happened to the cleaning? Everything's filthy! Nothing's packed! The place looks like a bombsite. Does Dad think he'll wave a magic wand and it'll all happen?"

"Something like that," Jeff said. "He'll get movers

to put everything in storage and then the commercial cleaners will come."

"What?" Her eyebrows came together. "Let's get this straight. Everything goes into storage? So what's put into the house we're renting?"

"We're not renting a house. Not yet." He saw her frown deepen and he felt uncomfortable. "Dad says he doesn't know what kind of house Mum wants. So we're going to go to a motel for a few weeks."

"Which one?"

Jeff looked at the floor. "The Market Motel."

"The same as Mum?" She gave an explosive laugh. "The cunning old fox! You have to admit it – he's a trier. Does Mum know?"

He shook his head.

"I'll bet she doesn't. As soon we move in, she'll move out. What's he thinking of?"

"I don't know," said Jeff. "He's a bit lost without her."

"He's hitting the bottle," Andrea said. "I could smell it as soon as I walked in, and he looks awful."

"He'll be better now you're home, Andy. He's missed you."

His sister gave him a hard look. "Don't you start!"

"Start what?"

"Emotional blackmail. Right now, you can pull the plug on your computer, little brother, and do some real work. You and I are going to clean up this disgusting place."

The thought gave him a good feeling, working together, Andy and Squidge like before. But there was something he had to do first. "You said you'd give me Beck's address," he told her.

* * *

Winston had left the newspaper on the concrete by his wooden chair. It was close to the low wall that overlooked the harbour, but the breeze was still catching it, flapping a triangle of pages. A good gust would take it apart and spread it over the garden. Jeff went out to get it. He had been cleaning windows and was wearing purple gloves that were too big. He had to take them off to open up the paper on the table. This time, she was in the obituary column. He put his finger on the notice, Eleanor May Caldwell, age 89 years, funeral Aurora chapel. His finger stopped. This afternoon. The funeral was at three o'clock today!

He took the newspaper through to Andrea, who was dragging a mop over the white marble floor. "Look! It's the old lady, Andy. She died."

At first she didn't understand and he needed to fill in details. She took the paper from him and read the notice. "Eighty-nine. No wonder she was a sandwich short of a picnic."

"Her funeral's this afternoon," he said. "I want to go."

"Why?" She looked puzzled.

It was too difficult to explain, not here and in the middle of house cleaning. "I just want to. I have to, and I need you to come with me. Please, Andy."

"Why on earth would I go to the funeral of someone I don't know?"

"But I know her. Andy, I've never been to a funeral. I don't want to do it on my own. Please! We owe it to her."

"Because she came here in the storm? Oh Squidge! We don't owe her anything. I hate funerals."

He took the paper from her. "All right," he said, "I'll go on the bus."

She snatched the paper back. "Where is it? Aurora chapel?"

"It's in Newtown."

"All right, all right." She smiled in defeat. "You know why I came back here instead of staying with Mum? Of course you know. Because you are here! My squidgy little brother! So yes, bow down and thank me. I'll take you to the funeral, but we'll make it quick – there, in, out and back. Okay?"

"Okay," he said. "Cool! Thanks a million, Andy." He stepped forward to hug her, but she had already turned away to mop the floor.

They would leave in an hour. He guessed it was wrong to feel excitement about a funeral, but there was no other word for it. He looked at the sky above the harbour, a blue that went on beyond seeing. He imagined Maisie, free as air, up there, waving her stick at him. Or perhaps there were two Maisies, both of them laughing. Or maybe none at all.

* * *

Andrea drove and Jeff directed her. She didn't ask him how he knew where the Aurora retirement flats were, probably, he thought, because she wasn't interested. Her concerns about Maisie were history. She had other things on her mind. He knew that. He also knew that she was doing this just for him, and that filled him with warmth. Usually, his sister made promises and then forgot about them. This wasn't a promise. It was a sudden gift.

Her little car bumped over the rough driveway, past the green, box-like apartments, around the corner past the hospital, to a car park near a small building that had one word on a sign: *CHAPEL*. There was a black hearse in front of the building and two cars in the park.

"Not a big funeral," Andrea said. "Hardly anyone."

But she was wrong. The chapel was almost full, most of the people elderly, some in wheelchairs or with walking frames, and younger ones who would no doubt be the caregivers. He recognised the receptionist who had taken him to Maisie's room.

Andrea was surprised. "How did they all get here?"

"They live here," he whispered back.

Heads turned as they walked in. They sat in the back row near the aisle, and Jeff could see a wooden coffin on a stand, up front. It had a bunch of flowers on it. Some music was playing, the soft kind you heard in supermarkets, and there was a little pond with a fountain that trickled, though not in time to the music. He worked out the difference by tapping to the music with one hand, and the rhythm of the fountain with the other. He wondered if dead people could still hear things. Maybe spirits hung around to listen to what people said about them at their funerals. But that wouldn't be so for Maisie, who had crossed over weeks ago. He guessed that the dream-keeper wouldn't be hanging around, either.

After a while, his fingers stopped tapping the edge of his chair. The music had also stopped. In the room the air was so still it seemed that everyone was holding their breath, although they weren't. He could hear them. Old people breathing. Louder than the splashing water.

A man in a dark suit came out from behind a curtain and started talking about Miss Eleanor May Caldwell, and then other people seated in the rows came forward and had turns talking about Maisie. The nurse who had been by the bed described her as a woman who celebrated life right to the end. "She knitted bonnets for newborn babies and taught us all to play poker. She wasn't well, but she'd go out on her own and have all the staff looking for her. Once she got lost in a rainstorm and was taken to the public hospital. The next day she turned up at her unit, wearing a hospital gown and a towel. She'd simply walked out."

People laughed. It seemed everyone knew the story.

"We had some explaining to do," said the nurse. "But then that was Maisie. No one could give her orders. During World War Two she was in the air force in England, a bomber pilot who never got off the ground. She taxied those big aircraft around the airfields and ran up the engines for the pilots who'd fly them."

A man pushed his walker forward and tapped the microphone, even though he knew it was working. "She could have a tongue sharp as a pick-axe, our Maisie. I took her some flowers once, and she told me to take a long walk off a short jetty."

There was a roar of laughter and Jeff guessed the old people knew he wasn't telling it all. The man grinned and pretended to look embarrassed. Then he said, "You had to hand it to her. She was a great storyteller."

Jeff listened intently. Now he wondered if the dream-keeper was really Maisie making up a story.

That could be. The things she'd told him had made a fantastically good story and parts of it slid over into his truth. He glanced at Andrea to see how she was reacting. She wasn't. She had her head down, her phone out, and was texting someone. He hoped it wasn't Mark.

Someone said that Maisie had pulled the flowers out of the unit gardens so she could plant vegetables. Someone else talked for a long time about Maisie's involvement with the Labour Party. Finally, the man in the suit came back to the funeral speech. He had opened a book and was reading from it. "Once again Jesus addressed the people: 'I am the light of the world. No follower of mine shall wander in the dark; he will have the light of life …'"

Light, she had told him. Hold on to the Light.

People stood up to sing Maisie's favourite song, "Beautiful Isle of Somewhere". Jeff had not heard it before, but he stood up and so did Andrea. His sister gave him a strong nudge. "Let's get out of here before they start asking questions about who we are."

* * *

As they drove away from the chapel, Andrea said, "Now you know what a funeral is like. Satisfied?"

"Yes. Oh yes! I'm glad you took me, Andy."

"The mourners usually go somewhere afterwards for refreshments. Sandwiches, cups of tea, heaps of talk. We couldn't do that."

"I know," he said, glad she had steered him away.

"It's nearly five. If you're hungry we can stop for Chinese."

"No. We'd better get back to the cleaning." But really, he was thinking of Winston who would be sitting in the wooden chair, a bottle beside it, staring out over the harbour.

At the top of the hill, he pressed the release button, the bronze gates opened inwards, and Andrea drove to the front of the garage. He got out and ran into the house while she put her car away.

His father was not in his usual place, which didn't surprise him because the sun had disappeared and the air was now cold. He would be in his office. "We're home, Dad!" he called, unzipping his jacket.

There was no reply. He walked through to Winston's office. The light was on, the computer humming, but his father wasn't there either.

"Dad?" he called. "Dad, are you home?"

That's when he heard the noise, a long grunt that sounded strained. He ran into his parent's bedroom. Winston was lying on the floor, one eye almost closed, the other wide open and rolling. "Ugh! Ugh!" He was wearing shorts and a grey striped shirt. A clawed hand reached towards Jeff and then fell back on the floor. There was spit coming from his mouth as he struggled to talk. "Ugh!"

Jeff ran from the room, yelling, "Andy! Andy!"

* * *

Andrea was right. It was a stroke. The ambulance people wheeled in a stretcher, lifted Winston onto it, and cranked it up as high as a bed. They didn't take him out immediately. They gave him an injection and unbuttoned his shirt to listen to his heart. They stuck patches on his chest and plugged in wires connected to a machine. They put an oxygen mask over his nose. He kept making grunting noises and the open eye, rolling from one person to another, was still wide with fear. Jeff moved forward and took his father's hand between his, but he was in the way of the paramedic and he had to drop the hand and step back beside his sister.

Helen must have left immediately after Andrea's phone call because she arrived while Winston was still in the house. It was just as well, because she could answer the paramedic's questions. Only she knew the details. Who was Winston's GP? Was he on any medication? Did he have health insurance? Helen looked calm, but her voice shook when she gave them information.

Now the wide-open eye was on Helen and

Winston was struggling to speak. With his good hand he tore off the oxygen mask and made a blubbering sound that oozed spit. Helen shook her head. "You stupid man!" she said, but she sounded more upset than angry.

The paramedics wheeled the stretcher out of the bedroom, down the white corridor and around the corner into the living room. Andrea and Jeff held the doors open. Helen followed behind.

It was dark outside. As they put Winston into the ambulance, Andrea said to one of them, "Can my brother go with him?"

The man looked at Jeff, but before he could say anything, Jeff turned to his mother. "Mum, you go in the ambulance."

She shook her head.

"He needs you!" His voice was strong. "You have to go!"

The man now looked at Helen.

She was trembling. "I can't leave the children."

Jeff grabbed her by the arm and steered her. "Mum! Go with Dad!" He heard his voice, loud like a strong wind blowing. "Stay with him! Andy and I will be fine."

"You can sit in the front with me," the paramedic told her.

Helen climbed in. The other paramedic got in the back with Winston and the doors closed. As the ambulance went out through the gates, Andrea said what Jeff was thinking. "She's more afraid than he is."

"He'll be all right, won't he?" Jeff asked.

She put her arm around his shoulders. "Of course he will. Strokes are nothing these days."

But he knew they were both thinking about the funeral, and the people with wheelchairs and crutches. It had felt so right to go there for Maisie, but if they had stayed home, Winston would have got help sooner. How could something be right and wrong at the same time?

That night he took out Andy's letter with the prison address and wrote five long pages to his brother.

* * *

Helen took leave from work and, although she didn't stay at the house, she came up each morning to organise things. In the afternoons they went to the hospital to sit with Winston.

For the first two days he was in the intensive care unit, in a network of tubes connected to machines and bags of fluid. He was sedated but he knew they were there. Helen sat close to him and held his good hand. "Sweetie, I need to know if you have booked a removal firm. Can you squeeze my hand once for yes, twice for no."

They all saw the hand move twice.

"That's two for no. Can you do that again to confirm? We don't want to double book. Excellent! Another no. We'll arrange it. Now, can we do the same for storage? Did you organise that? One for yes, two for no."

The doctor had told them that Winston was likely to get his speech back in a few days. In the meantime, his active hand was their means of communication. Helen slowly read a list of furniture removal companies. His hand did not move. "Does this mean you have no preference?" Yes.

"Should I choose?" Yes. "Good, sweetie. Now here are the storage companies. The cheaper ones are out of town."

Jeff thought it strange that this should be the first conversation between them after the weeks of silence, but he was glad that Helen had taken over, and he guessed it would be a relief for his dad.

Back home, they were all in a frenzy of cleaning out cupboards and drawers. Helen had bundles of plastic sacks, black for rubbish and green for things to go to the Salvation Army. "We are not paying storage for stuff we don't want!" she said. She stuck a timetable on the fridge, what each person had to do and when, to get ready for the movers next Thursday. There was no time off except for sleeping, eating and hospital visits, but at least Helen's focus on the house meant there was no dwelling on past arguments. The only negative comment came when she was tired, and it was small criticism. "I can't believe that you and your father did nothing," she said to Jeff.

Nothing? Was she talking about washing cups and sweeping floors? We were not doing nothing, he wanted to tell her. We were surviving.

* * *

Winston was moved into a ward with other stroke patients at various stages of recovery. He was still connected to a monitor but the rest of his tubes had gone. When they walked in on Wednesday afternoon, he was propped up in bed, a cup in his right hand. He drank the tea through a straw because his mouth was still partially paralysed.

He was always pleased to see them, but when he tried to talk, the words struggled to free themselves from a thick tongue and saliva ran down his chin.

Helen wiped his face with tissues. "You've got some new flowers. They're beautiful, sweetie. Where do florists get roses and tulips this time of the year? Did the staff send them from work?"

"Esha," he said. "Esha."

Jeff saw a card with the bouquet. "They're from Eddie. You know. The gardener."

"Eddie? Oh." Helen dabbed at Winston's mouth.

"That's nice." She put the tissue in the waste bag. "Well, we've finished. The house is clear for the removal people tomorrow. Tonight we're staying at the motel. We'll go back on Friday morning. A last flick of a duster, then I'll take the keys into the land agent. You have nothing to worry about. It's done."

He put down his cup and took her hand. "Shanku."

"The phone will be disconnected on Friday. I've cancelled newspapers, and, oh yes, Henry Sorensen is happy because he'll be continuing with the new owners."

Winston turned his head to Andrea and this time the word was clear. "School?"

She didn't know how to reply. She grinned awkwardly and said, "We're working on that, Dad."

When Winston smiled his face became a drama mask, one side comedy, the other tragedy. Jeff focused on the smile. He said, "Did Mum tell you the skinny detective came around yesterday?"

Instantly alert, his father turned to Helen.

"They've got him," she said. "Julius Clarke alias Warren Staunton-Jones was arrested in the south of France. He was wanted for fraud in several countries."

They did not tell Winston the rest of the news. The detective had said there was very little chance of recovering the money.

* * *

On Friday morning, Jeff stood by the low wall looking over the harbour that had small wind ruffles shimmering like blue silk. The garden furniture had gone but the rest of the garden was unchanged, small trees growing in concrete tubs, roses, herbs, the cactus bed, the swimming pool now with its cover locked down, the taller trees near the road neatly trimmed. The cut in the eucalyptus tree by the gate had healed over, but he still looked at it every time he went through; remembering the branch and the bundle of wet clothing with a white foot sticking out. That seemed years and years ago, but it was less than two months.

The morning was clear, no cloud to hide the fresh snow on the Kaikoura mountains on the other side of Cook Strait. The inter-island ferry crawled in the outer harbour. From this height it was like a white toy in a bathtub and he felt he could almost lean over the wall to pick it up. He would miss this view, but he would not miss the house. Now that all the furniture had gone, the house seemed to be its true self, an empty shell. It no longer had beds, tables and chairs and it did not have to pretend it was supposed to enclose people. The white walls, white arched ceilings and floors of white marble flecked with black all echoed emptiness. He wondered how the new family would fill it.

The Market Motel was okay. He and Andrea

had been there with Mum for two nights. He slept in the living area and they had twin beds in the bedroom. In the morning, they tripped over each other's bags, took turns in the bathroom and ate peaches with a spoon out of a can. It was messy and reminded him of the Fitzgibbon's place. As well, the motel unit had just one car park, so the two cars had to fit one behind the other. Fortunately, Andy's Toyota Vitz was small, but when the front car had to go somewhere, the back car had to let it out. He counted the number of times that happened.

He knew they would be in the motel until Winston was ready to come out of hospital. That could be several weeks, Helen said, because rehab took time. He had to learn to use the left side of his body and that didn't happen overnight. "Even when he does come out, he won't be fully mobile. Far from it! But you know your dad. He's very determined. He'll make it." Helen clapped her hands as certainty. "The house we buy will need easy access. No stairs."

Jeff noticed she no longer talked about "her house". She didn't mention any of that. It was as though the huge row had never happened. He was glad of that but found it very strange.

The inter-island ferry was now out in Cook Strait and Andrea was calling that it was time to go. Jeff turned. He didn't need to walk through the house.

Instead he walked around it, seeing the garden for the last time, and at the gum tree by the gate, he stopped to say goodbye.

★ ★ ★

The changeover went smoothly. Being right-handed, Winston could sign the papers in the rehab ward, and when the full payment for the house came through, he reinvested his clients' money in safe deposits. Doing that made a big difference to him. Helen remarked that it was as though he had dropped the world off his shoulders. He tackled his exercises with new energy and he was working on sentences rather than isolated words.

The other accountants from the office came to see him after work most days. They brought him work news and offered to smuggle in a good pinot noir or a bottle of single malt. Jeff hoped they were joking. His father had consumed no alcohol since the stroke and even the droopy eye was clear.

Helen brought him library books, but he could not concentrate for long and he preferred *Time* magazine, newspapers and some magazines about golf that Andrea bought for him.

One night, Andy announced out of the blue that she had changed her mind about law and wanted to do nursing. "Don't tell Dad," she said to Helen and Jeff. "He really wanted me to be a lawyer. I don't want to upset him."

Jeff shrugged. He thought their father would not be the least bit upset. He remembered when Maisie was under the gum tree, how Andrea had checked the old woman's pulse and told them to call the ambulance. His sister would make a great nurse.

* * *

Mrs Wilson was in fine form after the holidays. She bounced around the classroom telling the boys how much they had aged in the last two weeks without her, and how she had become younger without them.

"To get your grey matter working, here's a maths problem for you. It should appeal to the eggheads like Paul and Jeff." She leaned on her table. "There were three travelling salesmen who got caught in a storm. The road was flooded, they couldn't go on, and there was only one motel in the town. The sign outside said accommodation ten dollars."

"Ten bucks?" said Salosa. "That's unreal, man."

"This was years ago," Mrs Wilson said. "So the men asked for three rooms. The motel manager said, sorry, he had only one room left but it had three beds in it. It was better than nothing, so they each paid ten dollars and they were shown to the room."

Jeff wanted to laugh. Three people in one unit?

Mrs Wilson must be telepathic. Bet the salesmen were falling over each other, and there was a TV as big as a laptop screen on the wall!

"The manager was a decent bloke," said Mrs Wilson. "He looked at the thirty dollars and thought it was a bit much considering the men were all in one room. So he called the bellboy."

"What's a bellboy?" someone asked.

"He rings the school bell," someone else replied.

"He's the porter. He carries luggage and runs messages," said Mrs Wilson. "He calls the bellboy and gives him five dollars. He says, take the five dollars to the salesmen as a refund. But as the bellboy is walking to the room, he thinks, five dollars for three people is silly. He will give the men three dollars and keep the other two for himself. So in his pocket go two dollars. The other three go to the salesmen. Have you got that?"

"And that's a maths problem?" queried Paul.

"I haven't finished yet," she said. "Each of the men gets a dollar refund. They are very pleased. This means they've paid only nine dollars each. So here now is the problem. Nine times three equals twenty-seven. The bellboy has pocketed two. That makes twenty-nine. Where is the other dollar?"

"Huh? Will you repeat that, Mrs Wilson?"

She was enjoying this and her smile was huge. "Three men have paid nine dollars each. Twenty-seven dollars. The bellboy has two dollars. Twenty-nine. There is one dollar missing. Where is it?"

There were puzzled noises around the room, but Jeff knew the answer. He put up his hand. "The problem is the problem itself and the way you presented it," he said. "Even numbers can tell lies if they are worked out the wrong way."

* * *

Jeff went to the hospital after school. Winston was in a wheelchair by the window. His speech was still blurry, but he showed Jeff how he could squeeze a soft ball in his left hand. His walking was coming on, too. He could walk in the pool, and the physio nurses had him taking steps between two bars. "I'll be out of here soon," he said.

He had lost weight. When Jeff hugged him, he felt the bones of his father's shoulders and spine. He stood against the window and told Winston about school and Mrs Wilson's trick question. His father laughed, wiped his mouth and then asked about Helen. What time would she finish work? When was she coming? He saw her every day but he still asked. Jeff thought that maybe anxiety was part of the stroke.

There was something in Jeff that made him want to touch his father. He wanted to put his hand over the fingers that held the squeeze ball, straighten the collar of his pyjamas, put slippers on the feet softened by hospital living. They had never touched much before, but now that was different. Maybe it was the Light thing. Gladness filled Jeff when Winston reached up with his strong arm, put his hand over his son's head and dragged him over so that for an instant, their cheeks were pressed together.

This was the moment. Jeff said, "I've got a letter for you, Dad."

"Letter?"

"Can I read it to you?" He reached into his backpack.

"Sure. Go ahead." Winston wiped his mouth and tilted his head towards Jeff, who unfolded some handwritten pages.

Jeff moved closer. "*Dear Dad, Jeff told me about your stroke. I wanted to see you. I tried to get compassionate leave but my application was turned down. It failed, thank God, because you weren't dying. You were getting better. I want you to know that I miss you, I love you. You'd better believe that. Sometimes you have to go through hell to know what heaven is like. I'm sorry about the Sydney business. What a bummer! The good news is that I'm up for parole next year and if it's granted I'd like to be back somewhere near my family. I don't know how you feel about that …*" Jeff stopped reading and looked at his father.

Winston wasn't looking at him. He wasn't

looking at anything. His shoulders were shaking and water was running out of his eyes.

Slowly, Jeff laid the letter in Winston's lap. At that moment, it seemed to him that the hospital room was filled to the ceiling with Light.

11

PROPERTIES OF LIGHT: *Light will behave as waves in interference experiments, with two sets of waves interacting with each other to form a new pattern, just as ripples on a pond interact. In other experiments light will behave as a stream of fine particles called photons. In particle physics, photons are responsible for the electromagnetic force that we experience as light. Some matter – called dark matter – is believed to be unaffected by electromagnetism. This would mean that dark matter does not have a charge and does not give off light.*

Andrea was not going back to school. While she was wondering if she could, Helen phoned the school principal and was told, quite definitely, a return to class would not be possible. "She talked as though she had a mouthful of glass marbles," Helen said.

Jeff watched his sister. The old Andy would have fired up, but all she did was nod and continue to trim her fingernails. She had moved from packing shelves at the supermarket to working at the fresh fish counter, and this meant she had to have nails short and clean, her hair tucked under a white cap. She didn't seem concerned that she wasn't wanted back at college. "I'll do an online course," she said, examining her thumb.

"Such as?" asked Helen.

"Something that might be useful for nursing."

It turned out to be an online course on Community Health that Andy could manage with her supermarket job. "The topic is endless," she told Jeff. "There are so many factors – cultural, environmental, income, educational, age. I mean, you hear about child abuse, but did you know about elder abuse?"

Jeff thought of Maisie. Was it elder abuse for a dream-keeper to keep an old worn-out car on the road? He wasn't sure. There were a lot of things you couldn't put into words. Some of them, though, he was sure you could tell in a story.

* * *

Paul came to school with an announcement. The Fitzgibbons' dog had pups during the night. It had never occurred to Jeff that the mutt was a she. After all, its name was just Dog, which was quite original when you came to think of it. Not many dogs were called Dog. He went to Paul's place the next day, and in the laundry at the back of the house, Dog lay in a blanket-lined clothes basket with three squirming pups about the size of guinea pigs. Their eyes were closed and they made squeaking noises as they groped for the teats on Dog's front.

"Be careful," said Paul. "She's very protective."

But Dog looked at Jeff with clear, smiling I-know-you eyes and when he put out his hand, she licked his fingers.

"It's her first litter," Paul explained. "That's why there are only three."

Beck's number, thought Jeff.

"We don't know who the father is. Each one is different. The bigger black one was born first. Then came the one that looks like Dog, only she's got a black patch over one eye. The last was the black-and-white pup. Which do you like best? I like the big one."

Jeff squatted down by the basket. He studied the third pup with little white legs and stomach and a black saddle over its back. The fur was so short and fine, it showed pink skin, and the paws had tiny translucent claws. Number three, he was going to say. But then the second pup, the one most like its mother, crawled away from its food supply and blindly nuzzled his fingers. It was such a soft touch, he laughed with surprise.

"She's chosen you," said Paul.

He pulled his hand away. "I can't ever have a dog."

"I didn't mean that. But if you wanted her, it would be fine. We have to find homes for them."

Of course, he wanted her. All his life he had wanted a dog, but that was like wanting the moon. "We're in a motel."

"But you're going to be in a house, and the pups won't be ready for at least four months."

"It's not that. It's my parents. They've never had animals and they −" He stopped. The topic had a history too heavy to bring up in conversation. He was glad when Paul's mother came to the door to tell them she had taken some empanadas out of the oven. Were the boys hungry?

They sat at the kitchen table with Rosa and Teresa, and Mr Fitzgibbon came in, wiping rain off his glasses, saying he'd been at the post office when a whiff of empanadas had called him home. He took off his wet jacket and sat down, but before he bit into the hot meat pastry he said to Jeff, "So you've seen the puppies?"

Jeff knew then that the idea of him having one of Dog's puppies had already been discussed. A great sadness squeezed his chest. "They're nice," he said.

Paul looked at his father. "Jeff's not allowed to have a dog."

Mr Fitzgibbon did not seem surprised or

disappointed. He simply changed the subject. "Your dad's doing well. He thinks he'll be out in a week or two."

Jeff knew about the visit. Winston said he and Jim Fitzgibbon talked about golf, the best place to go for a car wash and the New Zealand horses in the Melbourne Cup.

"Anything new on the house front?" Mr Fitzgibbon asked.

Jeff chewed, swallowed and had some orange cordial. He liked Mrs Fitzgibbon's South American food, but didn't know why chilli sounded cold. He put the glass down. "Mum's given up looking for a house to rent. There was nothing with wheelchair access. Now we're going to buy."

"That sounds like a good idea," said Mrs Fitzgibbon. "Moving house is hard work. Why do it twice?"

"Mum's looked at a house in Lyall Bay. It's old but on flat land and we can get a ramp built for Dad. Mum showed Dad photos and he told her, go ahead." He looked at the table and wondered if he should say the next bit. "The house — it's got four bedrooms."

No one said anything, but they smiled. That meant they understood one day Beckett would be living with them.

He went on eating. The hot peppers with the silly name tasted okay.

* ★ ★

The house was perfect. The land agent said it was eighty years old, but Jeff knew that it had to be eighty-one. Yes, eight and one! The sun-baked bungalow with flaking white paint on the windowsills was surely a nine. Only two blocks back from the beach, it sat on a little section, mostly sand held down by a variety of wild grasses and succulents. It had low wooden fences that allowed a view of the neighbours' windows and clothes lines.

There was a white-painted garage with a green door, big enough for one car and a few garden tools. They could live with that, Helen said. The problem was the number of steps to the front door, because the house was built on high foundations to stop sand coming inside. A ramp would definitely be needed, but if the owner accepted their offer, Eddie and François would come in and build it. Two days max, said Eddie when he called in at the motel to discuss it. Ramp finished before the old man would be out of hospital.

"Cool!" Jeff said to Eddie. "I'll help you at the weekend."

For Jeff, the two best things were the beach at Lyall Bay, with surfers riding its waves, and the inside of the eighty-year-old house. An extra bathroom with a disability shower had been added at the back, but the rest was really old, with wooden panelling on the living room walls and varnished doors. There were cork tiles on the kitchen floor, blue carpet in the bedrooms, and white plastic light shades hanging on cords in the centre of each room. The house smelled of sunshine and old wood and saltiness, as though the sea had once sneaked in during the night.

He breathed in deep. Yeah! He would get a surfboard!

The back bedroom by the kitchen was his. He stood in it, letting the walls wrap themselves around him. He could have his bed here and his desk there, and there would still be space left over. It was a story, of course. Not true, but he could make it up, a basket in the corner with a patch-eyed puppy. It was all right to imagine running a dog along the beach, throwing sticks in the water, okay as long as you knew it could never happen. For that matter, even the house might not happen, if someone else bought it first.

He opened and closed the wardrobe door. If there was a patch-eyed puppy in a basket, he would call it Maisie. That name was a two.

* * *

In the rehab unit, Winston had traded pyjamas for track pants and a T-shirt, and he spent much of each day in a large armchair with an overhead hoist. He could now get out of the chair by himself, walk three steps with his walking frame, turn, then go back to the chair. "I do that every hour," he told Helen. "What do you think about that?"

"Sweetie, you're wonderful!" Helen kissed his forehead. "I don't think I'd have the patience."

"Bloody hell," he growled. "I've got to do something while I'm waiting for your visit. How did the shifting go?"

"Nearly finished," she said. "I don't know what we'd have done without Eddie and François. They trucked in everything from the storage unit and put it in place."

"Everything?"

Helen laughed. "Less than half! How did we collect so much stuff? I suppose the rest can stay in storage until we decide what to do with it."

Winston dabbed at his mouth with his handkerchief. "Don't worry about it now. When I come home we'll sell it. No point in paying rental for surplus furniture." He turned his head to Jeff. "And how's Jeffrey our mathematician? Counting all the streets between the new house and the hospital?"

Jeff shrugged. His father's smile was lopsided but it was good to see. "It's a long way from your office, Dad."

"I'll be working from home for a while." Winston gave a one-shoulder shrug. "Maybe back on my feet by summer."

"You'll be playing golf again by summer," said Helen, but they all knew that wouldn't be true.

They were quiet for a while, and then Winston reached out with his strong hand and took hers. "It's been one hell of a ride, honey."

"I know," she said. "But you've made an amazing recovery."

"I mean all of us." He shook her hand from side to side. "That southerly storm and the homeless woman. It started then, didn't it? What the hell happened?"

Helen pulled back her hand and placed it on top of his. "No, Wins, it started before that. Mr Staunton so-called Jones! I hope they make him eat his filthy money!"

Jeff wanted to say that it started earlier, with lots of things, the way they were about Beckett, and even before that. Maisie called it something. Forgetting the memory of Light, she said. But telling them would be way out of order. "There are good people in the world," he said. "Kind people who've helped us."

"Too damned right, Jeffrey." Winston laughed. "Look at the support we've had! Anyway, storms have their uses. They say a calm sea never makes a good captain."

Jeff remembered Beck's letter to their father, and the comment about knowing hell to appreciate heaven. He supposed it meant the same thing. Somewhere in a box of papers he had the notes he'd made of his last conversation with Maisie. He would try to find them. Some of that stuff about people choosing paths was making sense.

* * *

They were going to Auckland! Jeff was so excited that he sometimes found himself holding his breath, either with eager anticipation or else with apprehension. He would be seeing his brother. But would Beck be different? He looked different in the newspaper photo, although he sounded the same in his letters.

Jeff started counting things again, unimportant things, like the leaves on the geranium plant by the car park, the number of baked beans on his toast. He timed Mrs Wilson's lessons to the nearest second and turned them into a graph. It helped, although he didn't know why. It just seemed that numbers made his breathing easier.

The flight was booked for the week Winston came out of the rehab ward. The doctor said it was too early for travel, but he didn't know Helen was a senior employee of a big travel firm that would make the journey easy.

An attendant wheeled Winston to the plane, where a front aisle seat was reserved for him. Helen sat next to Winston and Andrea had the window seat. Jeff was in the seat across the aisle. He waited until the attendant had gone, then he leaned across. "The Boing 737 has one hundred and thirty-three seats," he told his father. "The old Fokker Friendship had only twenty-eight seats."

"Not now Jeffrey," said Helen.

Jeff saw that his dad had closed his eyes and was looking tired, much older than fifty-three. Strokes did that to people. But they got better. They did. They got extremely well again, and when his father turned fifty-four, his nine number, he would be in perfect health.

It was a good thought to hold.

Andy seemed older, too. Because she was tall, she'd always looked more than her age. She still acted young, though. Now it was as though the inside had caught up with the outside. Jeff missed his sister's laughter and mad singing. But she'd be eighteen in another month. She would be a nine number, and that was a good thought, too.

Jeff sat back in his seat. He couldn't wait to talk to Beck. He'd probably have to wait to tell his brother about Maisie. Beck would understand the notes about dream-keepers and Light and dreams. He'd know all that stuff.

In Auckland, there was light rain from fat clouds squashed down on buildings. Andrea held an umbrella over the wheelchair while Helen pushed Winston out to the taxi rank. Jeff carried his mother's bag.

Helen had organised a disability van with a hoist. Winston was picked up in his chair and then clicked into place inside, next to Andrea and Jeff. Helen sat in the front.

The van driver had glasses that sat low on a lumpy nose. He said he would wait for them at the prison car park and take them back to the airport for the flight home. He turned to Helen. "You won't be able to take that handbag in, love. Strict, they are. You'll all be searched. Wheelchair, too. Got your visitors' papers?"

"We've done all that," said Winston.

"My husband's medication is in this bag," said Helen.

The driver laughed. "You know how many times they've heard that one? Don't worry. The bag's safe in the van. If Mr Lorimer needs anything you'll have to bring him out. No exceptions. Everyone gets treated the same."

Jeff's heart beat so fast, he could feel it in his ears. He had seen movies of prison visits where people sat at tables in a room like a large cafeteria without food or drink. He wondered if they would all be allowed around a little table, or if they would have to go in one by one. But this was different.

The guard, a large woman with thin eyebrows, took them into the family room. It looked a bit like the waiting room in the stroke unit: metal chairs; two small tables, one with magazines; and bright fluorescent lights in a low white ceiling. They were told to sit and wait.

Helen remained standing, twisting the rings on her left hand. Jeff knew she was anxious about leaving her bag in the van. It was hard to trust a smiling man, after Mr Warren Staunton-Jones. "I didn't get the driver's name," she said.

Winston said, "If it goes missing, I'll get you a new one."

She laughed then, and sat down. "Where's Beckett? Everything smells of pine disinfectant. Comb your hair, Jeffrey. It's a mess."

"Let him be." Winston waved his strong hand. "His hair's fine. He's a good-looking kid. When I was his age, I was as ugly as sin. Now look at me." He grinned at her. "Handsome as hell!"

She grabbed his hand and squeezed it.

Jeff didn't laugh at the joke. His stomach still felt as though bugs were crawling in it. He started counting the seconds because there was nothing else to count. But the moment he had been waiting for was close.

At forty-seven there was a noise outside and at forty-eight the door opened. A man came in, a tall, thin version of Winston. He had hair like hay stubble and deep lines at the edges of his mouth. But the eyes were as Jeff remembered them, a pale blue that caught the light and held it.

Before any of them could stand up to greet him, the guard came in and closed the door. Beckett sat down in the chair between his father and Andrea. He looked at them and his eyes twitched. "You're here. All of you. Thanks for coming."

There was a silence. It wasn't easy to talk with the guard standing against the door. Helen twisted her hands. "You don't look like – You're so thin!"

"Yeah." Beckett glanced down at himself. "I had amoebic dysentery last year. I'm putting on weight now, working in the kitchen. He ran his hands down the front of his shirt and then smiled, his head still down. "You've all changed, too."

"Not for the better, in my case." Winston indicated his weak arm.

Beckett looked up then. He put his hand on his father's shoulder. "These situations are temporary, Dad. Everything passes." He turned. "Time! So much time! Andy, you're a beautiful woman. Jeff! My little Mr Number Freak, you're sprouting like a runner bean! Thanks for the letters. Both of you." He changed direction and put his face close to Helen. "Mum, you've changed the least. I like that grey in your hair. Looks classic."

Jeff glanced at the guard standing against the door. He was Samoan, maybe, black curly hair, and he looked straight ahead, no expression at all. Did he have a family that talked like strangers? Jeff licked his dry lips. This was the meeting he'd longed for. He should be happy.

Helen folded her hands in her lap. "We've moved into our new house and we –"

Winston interrupted. "Your mother did all the work. Her and Andrea and Jeffrey." He put his handkerchief to the corner of his mouth. "I was sitting on my backside in rehab."

"Yeah." Beckett smiled with one side of his mouth. "I know a bit about rehab."

"This kind of rehab is different," said Winston. "We do these confounded exercises, in the pool, out of the pool, walking between two bars –"

Helen nudged him. "Beckett knows it's different."

Winston wiped his mouth again and shrugged with one shoulder. "Okay, okay."

They all laughed. Jeff too. He didn't know what else to do. Under the laugh, he counted his heart beats, averaging eight to every breath. Helen continued, "The house has four bedrooms. Beckett, one of them is yours."

Jeff stopped breathing.

Beck's smile disappeared and his eyes widened, a transparent blue. "Really?" It was almost a whisper.

"Bloody hell, yes," shouted Winston, punching Beckett on the shoulder. "It's been a bloody awful year."

Andrea looked quickly at the guard. "Dad, don't swear!"

"I'll bloody well swear if I want to. It's been a rough road, but we're family, aren't we? If family can't hang together, what else can we do?" He pointed across the room at Jeff. "That boy has been bloody marvellous. You'd better believe it. That one's been the glue in the family."

Jeff took a deep breath and felt his chest expand. He had been thinking about all he would say when he saw Beck again, but so far he had not been able to find a single word.

"Don't know where we'd be without him," Winston said to Beckett. "We've done the unthinkable. We've arranged to get him a puppy."

What? Jeff sat upright, but only for a second. Like hell, they were getting a puppy.

Winston could put promises in reverse faster than a car. Unthinkable! Fleas, hydatids, rabies, filthy bloody mongrels!

"Oh, sweetie!" cried Helen. "That was supposed to be for his birthday!"

Winston was pointing at Jeff. "One of Jim Fitzgibbon's pups. The one you like."

Forgetting the guard, Jeff sprang off his chair,

bounded three steps across the room and stopped. It couldn't be true. It was a trick. He stood in front of his parents. "But you hate dogs!"

They laughed. That was their response, bursts of laughter, happy, loud, rising and falling. He hadn't said anything funny, but it went on and on. All of them laughing, like waves of light, Helen, Winston, Beckett, Andrea and finally, himself. Yes, definitely himself! They were all over their heads, drowning in laughter, because it was true. They meant it! Everything was true! And then with the laughing, the rest happened, first Beckett up out of his chair and swinging Jeff around, hugging him against his prison shirt. Spinning around and around! Andrea with them, kissing him, kissing Beck, weeping into the laughter, and Helen getting in the middle, hugging them all, with her lipstick smudged, her hair over her eyes. Then all four were leaning over Winston's chair, smothering him with hands and kisses, and laughing with some tears and some swearing. They were awash with Light!

It was very fast, as though all the terrible things that had happened were suddenly a huge joke that swept them together in a heap of family and although there were no numbers to count, Jeff knew the moment was perfect.

THE END

A NOTE FROM THE AUTHOR

I developed the idea for this novel over three years, from reading that went back a lot further. When I was writing the book, I gathered information from a variety of sources. Some of the reading came from the mystical traditions of several religions, while others came from books and the internet.

I would like to particularly acknowledge the following sources:

Dr Quantum Presents: A User's Guide to the Universe by Fred Alan Wolf (audiobook, 2005, Colorado: Sounds True)

Thinking in Numbers: On Life, Love, Meaning, and Math by Daniel Tammet (2012, London: Hodder and Stoughton)

Wonders of Numbers: Adventures in Mathematics, Mind, and Meaning by Clifford Pickover (2001, New York: Oxford University Press)

The Pan Dictionary of Mathematics (1990, London: Pan)

New Zealand Sailing Guide; New Zealand Boatmasters' Course; Aoraki Polytechnic Certificate in Woodturning course notes

Encyclopaedia Britannica

Wikipedia.org (accessed February 13, 2014), with special acknowledgement for the following chapter openings:

Chapter 3: "Black hole,"
http://en.wikipedia.org/w/index.php?title=Black_hole&oldid=595309620

Chapter 4: "Prime number,"
http://en.wikipedia.org/w/index.php?title=Prime_number&oldid=593374659

Chapter 6: "Sound,"
http://en.wikipedia.org/w/index.php?title=Sound&oldid=595995385

Chapter 8: "Fibonacci number,"
http://en.wikipedia.org/w/index.php?title=Fibonacci_number&oldid=595209997

Chapter 9: "Tide,"
http://en.wikipedia.org/w/index.php?title=Tide&oldid=596074112

Chapter 10: "Terminal velocity,"
http://en.wikipedia.org/w/index.php?title=Terminal_velocity&oldid=596178967

Chapter 11: "Photon,"
http://simple.wikipedia.org/w/index.php?title=Photon&oldid=4618327

and my husband Terry who is at home in the world of math and physics.

BUSSELTON SENIOR HIGH SCHOOL

LIBRARY